BRAZEN BARTER

A Voion shot across their path and brought a handgun up just as Fufu veered to slam him under his wheels. Another Voion fired at Retief, who ducked, thrust with his sword, saw the Voion wobble wildly, go over, bounce high, and slam into a tree.

Suddenly the Voions retreated. A Voion flying wagon approached.

"Tief-tief!" the newcomer called, lifting off a hollow headpiece to reveal a pale grey face and five eyestalks. "We have in our custody ten Terry females, removed from a disabled vessel illegally on Voion soil. They are scheduled to be shot at dawn. I offer you their lives in return for the surrender of yourself!"

Books by Keith Laumer

The Best of Keith Laumer
Fat Chance
Retief and the Warlords
Retief of the CDT
Retief's War

Published by POCKET BOOKS

Keith Laumer

RETIEF'S WAR

PUBLISHED BY POCKET BOOKS NEW YORK

All of the characters in this book are fictitious, and any resemblance to actual persons, living or dead, is purely coincidental.

This science fiction novel was originally published in three parts in the *Worlds of If Science Fiction* magazine.

POCKET BOOKS, a Simon & Schuster division of
GULF & WESTERN CORPORATION
1230 Avenue of the Americas, New York, N.Y. 10020

Copyright © 1965 by Galaxy Publishing Corporation

Published by arrangement with Doubleday & Company, Inc.
Library of Congress Catalog Card Number: 66-17436

ISBN: 0-671-81863-5

First Pocket Books printing December, 1978

10 9 8 7 6 5 4 3 2 1

Trademarks registered in the United States and other countries.

Printed in the U.S.A.

RETIEF'S WAR

1

Jame Retief, Second Secretary and Consul of the Terrestrial Embassy to Quopp, paused in his stroll along the Twisting Path of Sublime Release to admire the blaze of early morning sunlight on the stained glass window of a modest grog shop wedged between a stall with a sign in jittery native script announcing Bargain Prices in Cuticula Inlays, and the cheery façade of the Idle Hour Comfort Station, One Hundred Stalls, No Waiting. He took out a long cigar of the old-fashioned type still hand-rolled on Jorgensen's Worlds, glanced back along the steep, narrow street. Among the crowd of brilliantly colored Quoppina —members of a hundred related native species mingling freely here in the Great Market of Ixix—the four Terrans who had been trailing him for the past half hour stood out drably.

Retief drew on the cigar, savoring the aroma, turned and stepped through the low arch into the tavern. From a high stool within the raised ring-bar at the center of the gaily lit chamber, the barkeeper—a medium-sized, short-abdomened individual of the Herpp tribe, with chipped wing cases of faded baby blue and four dextrous arms of bristly wine-red on one of which a Terran wristwatch was strapped—manipulated the controls of the dispenser console, exchanged banter with the customers, made change, and kept a pair of eyes on the free lunch simultaneously. He saw Retief, tilted his anterior antennae in friendly greeting.

"I am Gom-Goo, and I dance the Dance of Welcome," he susurrated in Quopp trade dialect, his voice reminiscent of fingernails on a blackboard. "What'll it be, Retief?"

"I'm Retief, and I dance the Dance of Glad Arrival," the diplomat replied in the same tongue. "How about a shot of Bacchus brandy?"

"Red or black?"

"Black." The other customers made room as Retief moved up, unclipped a carefully charred wooden bowl from the serving panel, got it under the proper bright-plated nozzle just in time to catch the tar-colored syrup as it jetted forth.

"That's pretty good stuff," Gom-Goo said; he lowered his voice. "But for a real kick, you ought to try a shot of Hellrose—cut ten to one, of course. That'll put a charge on your plates."

"I tried it once. Too sweet for a Terry. We like our sugar fermented."

"Sourballs?" The Herpp indicated an assortment of pea-sized lumps of yellow, white, purple, and green.

Retief shook his head. "I prefer salt peanuts to salt-peter," he confided.

"Well, every tribe to its own poison."

"Here's oil in your crankcase," Retief toasted formally, nibbling the brandy.

"Oil," Gom-Goo responded. "You haven't been in lately, Retief. Been dormant?"

"No more so than usual, Gom-Goo. Ambassador Longspoon's been imposing non-union hours on the staff, I'm afraid. Wouldn't do to let the Groaci steal a march on us and get a Bolshoi-type ballet theater built before we can get a Yankee-stadium type sports arena off the drawing board."

Gom-Goo worked his dorsal mandibles in the gesture that expressed courteous skepticism. "Frankly, Retief, we Quoppina aren't much interested in watching Terries hobble around. After all, with only two legs and no wings . . ."

"I know; but it's traditional in these diplomatic competitions to build something conspicuously inappropriate."

Gom-Goo tilted his oculars toward the door, where a pair of Quoppina with highly polished black carapaces were rolling past, twirling nightsticks.

"Speaking of Terry programs, Retief, just between you and me, what's behind this business of buffing up these Voion ne'er-do-wells and setting them to cruising the streets waving clubs at the rest of us?"

"Well, Gom-Goo, it appears that in some quarters the view is held that you Quoppina are a little too fond of brawling, anarchy, and dueling in the streets to qualify as natural democrats. Ergo, a native police force."

"Uh-huh—but why pick the Voion for the job? Their tribe's made its living by waylaying honest Quoppina in back alleys ever since the Great Egg first hatched—"

A heavy foot clumped behind Retief. He turned to find the four Terrans ringing him in, ominous expressions on their weathered features.

"We're just in from the Trading Post at Rum Jungle," the lean, scar-faced member of the quartet said flatly. "We want to have a little talk with you, Mister." He put his left fist carefully against the palm of his right hand and twisted it, looking around nervously.

Retief nodded. "Go ahead," he said pleasantly. A large man with thick, protuberant ears and thin sandy hair eased the scarred man aside.

"Not in this dump," he said in a voice like a cannonball rolling downstairs. "Outside."

"If it's a private matter, maybe you'd better drop by my office—"

"We already been to the Embassy; talked to some bird named Magnan," the big man said. "He acted like his lace drawers was itching him; no joy there."

"Don't argue with this chump, Big Leon," a squatty fellow with a bluish chin and a steel front tooth advised. "Bring him along."

The bartender leaned over and buzzed sharply. "My name is Gom-Goo," he started. "I—"

"Better get your wiring checked, low-pockets," Scarface cut him off. "Sounds like you got a short in your

9

talk box." He jerked his head at Retief. "Let's walk, Mister."

"I haven't quite finished my drink," Retief said mildly. "Why don't you go stand outside; I'll be along presently."

The fourth man, yet to be heard from, edged closer. "Ah, sir, we have a problem," he began. "We—"

"Skip it, Jerry," Scar-face snapped. He hooked a thumb over his shoulder, glowered at Retief. "Outside, you, like Big Leon said."

"Sorry," Retief said. "Some other time, maybe."

Scar-face narrowed his eyes, reached a large-knuckled hand for Retief's collar; Retief leaned aside, caught the hand, and flipped it over, his fingers against the palm, his thumb against the scarred knuckles, doubled it back over the wrist. Scar-face went to his knees with a yowl. Retief tsked.

"A very poor lead, Lefty," he said reproachfully. "It's a good thing I wasn't an enemy of yours."

"Hey," the big man said, stepping in. "Let him up."

Retief looked at the wide face that topped his own six-three by an inch. "Why do they call you Big Leon?"

Big Leon set himself. "Put Seymour down and I'll show you," he grated.

Retief shifted his grip, lifted the scarred man clear of the floor, hoisted him chest-high. "Here, you have him," he offered, and tossed him at the big man. Leon staggered back, *oof!*ed, thrust Seymour aside, frowned, doubled a large fist, and moved in—

There was a shrill rasp of sound. A thick, five-foot Quoppina with a glistening black carapace decked out in elaborate silver ornaments rolled between Retief and Big Leon.

"Outside, foreign grubs!" the intruder keened. He waved a long billy club of black wood, jabbed it at the scar-faced man, who had stumbled to his feet. There were other club-wielders behind the first—two, three, half a dozen or more, all wearing the new black and silver trappings of the CDT-sponsored Federal Police. The Voion captain waved his palps, giving Retief a glimpse down a yellow-green throat set with silvery needles.

"All of you are under arrest," he rasped. "Place your manipulative members above your sense-organ clusters and proceed hence!"

10

"What's the charge?" Retief asked in the Voion dialect.

"Trespassing in forbidden territory, alien, not that it matters! The example may remind your fellows to remain in the ghetto graciously assigned to them by the indulgence of the Planetary Government!"

"Just a minute," the barkeeper interrupted from his perch above. "I am Gom-Goo and—"

"Silence, panderer to alien perversions," the Voion snapped. "Or I'll find dungeon space for you, too!"

The other Voion were unlimbering clubs now. Over their heads, Retief caught Big Leon's eye, jerked his head minutely to the right; the big man narrowed his eyes, nodded quickly. As the Voion before Retief brought his club back for a jab to the sternum, Leon reached, caught the alien by the upper pair of arms, lifted him clear of the floor, whirled him, and slammed him at his fellows. Two of them went over with a crash. Retief spun, intercepted an eager junior closing in from the left, caught him by his vestigial wing cases, sent him reeling back to collide with his partner as Scar-face feinted, twisted the club from the two-pronged grip of the nearest cop, ducked, and jammed it through the spokes of the alien's yard-high main wheels. The victim stopped with a screech and a twanging of broken spokes. Big Leon met a second charging Voion with a roundhouse swipe, yelled as his fist glanced off the armored and thorned thorax, then landed a blow that spun the creature aside. Retief, ready, spiked its main wheels with the club he had wrenched from his last victim, just as the sole undamaged Voion struck Big Leon a vicious blow behind the ear. Leon turned with a roar, picked up the cop bodily, and slammed him against the barkeeper's podium.

"Here!" the barkeeper shrilled. "I am Gom-Goo and I dance the Dance of Distress—"

"Let's get out of here!" Scar-face ducked aside as a Voion's club whistled, charged for the door. Quoppina of all sizes and colors scattered before him. Leon aimed a blow at a cop renewing the attack; Jerry took the arm of the fourth Terran, staggering from a bloody cut across the scalp, plunged through the crowd. Retief, backed against the podium by the last two Voion still in action, keeping their distance and swinging their clubs in whistling arcs, plucked a tall bottle from a display, got in a hearty crack

11

across the head of one as Gom-Goo leaned down and laid the other out with a bung starter.

"Retief!" The Herpp called above the chatter of the clientele who had been enjoying the free show. "I am Gom-Goo and I dance the Dance of Apology—"

"This dance is on me," Retief panted. "I think I'd better be off now, Gom-Goo; sorry about the damage—"

"It was entirely the fault of these jacks-in-office," the bartender clashed his wing cases in agitation. "Interfering in a friendly dispute among cash customers! Tum-Tuk. . . ." He signaled to his two table waiters. "Haul these Voion troublemakers out into the alley, to survive or not, just as they please." He leaned over to eye the one Big Leon had thrown against the podium. "As for this fellow, stuff him in the incinerator. He's shouldered his last free citizen off the parking-ledge."

"We'd better dust, Mister," Leon said. "That Bug was a cop and he's got plenty of pals . . ."

There was a distant clanging of gongs.

"You'd best transfer the scene of your diversions elsewhere for the nonce, Retief," Gom-Goo called. "One of these spoil-sports has summoned his fellow black-guards. . . ."

"We were just leaving; and thanks for tapping that last fellow; he was getting too close for comfort."

"My pleasure, Retief. The rascals have been getting pushier by the day. They're up to something, mark my words! And remember: After the wheels, the juncture between the parietal plates is the best spot to go for on a Voion."

"I'll remember that. Ta ta."

In a quieter grog shop half a mile from the scene of the action, Retief and four Terrans found a table at the back of the room from which they could keep an eye on the street. Through the wide, doorless arch, Voion cops could be seen hurrying past, grim and businesslike in their black and silver trappings. Big Leon blew on his skinned fist, looked at Retief almost shyly.

"Sorry about the rough stuff, uh, Mister, uh . . ."

"Retief. No apology needed. I see now why they call you Big Leon."

Leon nodded. "You looked pretty good in there yourself, Mister. Maybe those Bugs'll think about it before they tackle a bunch of Terries again."

"What's got into them Bugs?" the scarred man demanded. "They been giving us a hard time out in the field, but I figured they'd be minding their manners here in town."

"That's what we came here to talk about," Big Leon said. "Something's stirring the Voion tribe up. I thought it was just us planters and traders they were out to get, but they've got the whole town sewed up like a dead sailor."

"We pretty near didn't get into the city," the steel-toothed man said. "There's a patrol around the port; a man could get the idea he wasn't welcome."

"The new police force was designed to bring law and order to Quopp," Retief said. "According to the official T.O. there are supposed to be no more than a hundred of them assigned to the city, with smaller detachments at the major trading towns."

"A hundred my uncle Edgar," Leon growled. "The whole town's swarming with 'em—and there must be another ten thousand between here and Rum Jungle."

"Yes, I'd say our friends the Voion have answered the call to civic duty in surprising numbers," Retief said.

"They say Longspoon's the one behind it," Scar-face said. "Sometimes I wonder whose side you CDT boys are on."

"The motivation of the diplomat is an engima that even his best friend, if he had one, would be hard put to define," Retief confided. "Technically, the Corps Diplomatique Terrestrienne is dedicated to the protection of Terran interests, Galaxy-wide. Of course, figuring out what those interests really are can get a little complicated."

"Like equipping local cops with clubs to pound Terry heads, using fees squeezed out of Terry businessmen," Seymour growled.

"What does the Corps want here, anyway?" Leon demanded. "Quopp was doing all right—with a little help from Terry free enterprises; then along comes a bunch of CDT Johnnies getting everything organized, and all of a sudden us Terries are undesirable aliens."

Retief refilled glasses. "Admittedly, some of the measures selected by our Chief of Mission may seem paradoxical at first glance. But that's just because you haven't entered into the spirit of the game. All of the measures Ambassador Longspoon has taken—restrictions on private enterprise by Terrans, establishment of the Planetary Police, free goods for the indigent, subsidies for Voion commercial enterprise, and the rest—are designed to bring peace and plenty to the downtrodden locals whom you fellows have been exploiting."

"What do you mean, exploiting?" Big Leon's fist hit the table. "Why, a hundred years ago, when the first Terries hit Quopp, there was nothing here but wild Bugs living in grass huts and eating each other. We laid out the towns, built trails, started 'em in on a little cottage industry and intertribal trade. We brought in electronics men to be country G.P.'s, developed new lines of merchandise to make life more beautiful for the Quopp in the street, and taught 'em the idea of civilization. Sure, we made a good profit—but they've got their money's worth every step of the way!"

"Still, Leon, now that you've put Quopp on the star maps, competition has set in. Our friends the Groaci aren't going to let this world drift into the Terry camp without a struggle. They've set up a string of trading posts along the other coast of Continent One, and they're doing a brisk trade in miniature Tri-D's, artificial limbs and wheels, and electronic Mah-Jongg sets—"

"Direct competition with us!" Jerry burst out. "The copy-cats!"

"Of course," Retief went on, "no self-respecting diplomat could let the challenge pass without making an effort to out-enlighten the opposition. Whatever the Groaci do, we have to do bigger—"

"Why?" Seymour grunted.

"Why does a golfer have to hit the golf ball?" Retief riposted. "Such is the challenge of diplomacy."

"But why this sudden compulsion to unite the planet under a single government—and with the Voion in charge, of all people!" Jerry looked indignant.

"You know we can't even travel inland to look over the markets?" Big Leon said.

"You know why? The Voion! They're all over like a

14

land-lubber's lunch—waving clubs and telling *us* where we can and can't go!"

"Longspoon's making a mistake, backing the Voion," Big Leon said. "There's not a Bug on the planet doesn't hate their main windings. Slaves and dope-runners, con artists, highway robbers, and second-story men—that's what they were—until this idea of reforming 'em and putting badges on 'em came along."

"His Excellency envisions the day when a trained cadre of reformed Voion will lead the newly enlightened masses to a new era of planetary unity," Retief explained. "Or so he frequently says."

"Retief, how long you been here on Quopp?" Leon inquired.

"Only a few weeks, I'm afraid."

"You talk the dialects pretty good."

"I've spent a few hours on the encephalotapes."

"Uh-huh," Leon nodded. "Well, I was born here, Retief. Hell, I haven't been off the planet half a dozen times in my life. And I can tell you—these devils have got something up their sleeve!"

"I'm inclined to agree their police badges seem to have gone to their heads—"

"It ain't just that," Seymour said. "There's something in the wind! We saw it, out in the jungle—and now here in town! It's getting ready to pop! Pushing Terries around —that's bad medicine, Mister!"

"And I'll tell you something else," the steel-toothed man said. "Those Bugs are tapping CDT shipments at the port—in broad daylight!"

Retief frowned. "You're sure of that?"

"Been down to the port lately?" Big Leon inquired.

"Not in the past month."

"Come on," Leon rose. "Let's go take a look-see. There's a CDT shipment on the pad right now big enough to put half the Terries on Quopp out of business." As he stood, a buzzing three-inch yellow-green flyer sailed by, settled to a puddle of spilled liquor on the floor. Big Leon raised a size thirteen shoe—

"Don't do it," Retief said. "He probably needs a drink as bad as we did."

"That's just a Phip," Seymour said. "You talk like they was human."

"You never can tell," Retief said, skirting the small creature. "He just might be somebody's cousin George."

Outside, the five Terrans hailed two massive peach-colored Wumblums, mounted to the creaking velvet-lined seats strapped to the heavy creatures' backs, relaxed as their mounts trundled off on broad leather-shod wheels toward the space port, groaning up the steep slopes, puffing down the declines, shouting for way among the thronging Quoppina packing the route. Clear of the main shopping streets, the Wumblums made better time, wheeling along briskly under the crisp morning sky. Overhead, the glaring crescent of Joop, Quopp's sister world, swung toward its twice-daily eclipse of the distant sun, a blinding point of white light casting short midmorning shadows across the intricately surfaced buildings that thrust up everywhere like giant, lumpy loaves of pastel-toned bread.

"You gents coming back?" Retief's mount inquired in a voice like the E-string on a bass cello. It tilted an auditory receptor to pick up the reply over the noise of wheels on pavement. "Ten percent off for a round trip."

"Not right away," Retief said. "Better not wait for us."

"I'll stick around anyway; Voom-Voom's the name. Ask for me when you're ready to go. Not much action this morning. All these Zilk and Jackoo in town from the villages, they'd wear out their wheels rubbernecking before they'd hail a ride—and these Voion cops all over the place—they're not helping business any."

The Wumblum behind Retief's swung out, came along-side. "Looks like we got company," Big Leon called, pointing over his shoulder with a large, blunt thumb. Retief glanced back; a pair of Voion were trailing fifty yards behind, black shells glistening, light winking from their recently applied police insignia.

"There are two more flanking us on the right," Retief said. "I'd guess we're covered on the left, too. They don't want us to be lonely."

"Maybe you'd better cut out of here," Leon suggested. "I guess they're still mad. Me and the boys'll handle this."

"It's a nice day for a drive," Retief said. "I wouldn't think of missing it."

The Wumblum took a quick look back at Retief. "Some of those Voion giving you gents trouble?"

"They're trying, I'll concede that, Voom-Voom."

"Don't worry about a thing, boss. I'll say a word to my sidekick Rhum-Rhum, and we'll lead those grub-eaters down a couple of side streets to a cul-de-sac I know and work 'em over for you."

"That's friendly of you, old-timer, but we don't have time for any more horseplay today."

"All part of the service," Voom-Voom said.

The port came into view as the party emerged from the twisting avenue; a hundred acre expanse of hilly ground ringed by a sagging wire fence, paved and scabbed over with a maze of flimsy temporary structures, some now nearly a century old, among which the tall shapes of scattered vessels thrust up, festooned with service cables and personnel rigging. As Retief watched, a vast black shadow swept down the hillside beyond the ships, rushed across the port blanking out the gleam of sun on chromalloy and concrete and corrugated aluminum, then enveloped them, plunging the street into abrupt, total darkness. Retief looked up; the great fire-edged disk of Joop loomed black against the midnight blue sky. Voom-Voom lowered his head, and the beam of dusty light from his luminescent organ cut a path through the gloom ahead.

"You know, you Terries have done us Quoppina a lot of good," he said, slowing now to pick his way with more care. "Like the focusing lenses for us Wumblums' headlights; a real boon. And the rubber wheel-shoes like some of the fellows wear; a useful item. And the synthetic lubricants—and the surgical spares—you've kept a lot of fellows on the street earning a living at a time o' life when our dads would have been laid up for good. But these Voion cops, and this one-world, one-government idea: It's a mistake. It's always been every tribe for itself, and a good system, too—"

"Watch it, Retief," Big Leon called quietly. There was a soft swish of tires on clay pavement, the abrupt stab of yellowish light beams as fast-moving forms closed in on both sides.

"Halt!" a Voion accent came from the darkness. "Pull up here, you Wumblums, in the name of the law!"

"You small-time chiselers have got the gall to pull that routine on me?" Voom-Voom trumpeted, accelerating. "Stay out of my way, or I'll leave my tread-marks down your backs!"

"That's an order, you great bumbling lout!" One of the Voion, apparently carried away by his own recently acquired rank, swung too close; Voom-Voom shot out an arm like a ship-grapple, gathered the luckless creature in, tossed him aside to slam the pavement with a clang of metallo-organic body plates. A second Voion, veering aside, gave a shriek, disappeared under the massive wheels of Rhum-Rhum. The others sheered off, fell back, as the Wumblums sped off toward the lights now gleaming all across the port. Retief held on to the worn leather handstraps as the solid wheels hammered over the potholed road.

"A good thing the CDT hasn't gone as far as handing out power guns to those Jaspers," Seymour shouted as Rhum-Rhum came up on the starboard beam.

"Look there—" Jerry leaned forward beside Retief. "There are Voion swarming all over the port!"

"Don't worry, gents" Voom-Voom hooted. "Rhum-Rhum and me will stand by. That was the first time I've had my wheels on a Voion since the last time I caught one prying the lid off my fare-box. It felt good."

There was a flood-lit gate ahead, flanked by a pair of Voion who rolled forward officiously—and darted back as Voom-Voom barreled past them, slammed through the fence, hurtled on without slowing. They were in among the tall ships now, threading their way among stacked packing cases, dangling cargo nets, hurrying stevedores, and Vorch cargo-carriers, the latter squat Quoppina with three thick functional wheels and broad, labor-scarred carapaces. Ahead Retief saw the familiar CDT code stenciled on the sides of stacked cases being unloaded by Voion stevedores from the hold of a battered tramp trader under a battery of polyarcs.

"You notice they're not shipping the stuff in Corps vessels," Big Leon pointed out as their mounts pulled up at a signal from Retief. "It's all handled pretty cagey; looks like there's angles to this that Longspoon doesn't want publicity on. It just happens I know that cargo-mark."

A pair of bustliing Voion were at work on the cargo net, overseeing the placement of the crates. Others stood about, as though on guard—humbler specimens than the elite police, Retief noted; their dull black wing cases lacked the high polish and brightwork of their favored tribesmates. One, wearing the armband of a Ramp Master, wheeled across to confront the visitors. He was an oldster, beginning to silver around the edges, his thickened wing cases showing the marks of repeated paring.

"What d'ye seek here, sirs?" he chirped in tribal Voion, in what was meant to be an authoritative tone, meanwhile working his anterior antennae in frantic Voion thieves' code.

"Shift . . . cases . . . conceal . . . special . . . consignment . . ." Retief deciphered. He noted a sudden stir of activity among the Voion at the net. A pair of the patrolling stick-wielders rolled in to help. The center of attention appeared to be a stack of cases conspicuously tagged with large red cards reading "For the Terran Ambassador."

"We takee look-see," Seymour was saying in trade pidgin. "We lookee gift-gift Terry friend-friend send."

"Very good," the oldster shifted to the same tongue. "Looky see, plenty ski pants, snowshoe, smoked oyster, bagels, tennis racquet, paint-by-number kit; all stuff keep tiny Quoppina tot alive all winter."

"You hear that, Retief?" Big Leon growled. "Some of my hottest trade items, those are. You'd think Longspoon was deliberately trying to put us traders out of business." He pointed suddenly. "Hey, look there!" A Voion in tribal dress, with the feathery antennae of a Flying Jarwheel strapped to his head, was maneuvering a pink Timblum—a smaller cousin of the mighty Wumblum—into position. There was a squat cart hitched behind the mount.

"That's Smuk; he's a retired slaver; used to be one of my best customers. Now look at him, freeloading! No wonder I don't see him around the warehouse sales anymore!"

Retief climbed down from his seat, strolled across to study the stacked crates. The Ramp Master trailed him, his wheels squeaking on the dry bearings of old age. Behind the façade of hurriedly placed boxes, Retief counted at least half a dozen of the red-marked cases, identical with the others except for the prominent diplomatic address. The Voion twittered nervously at his heels.

"Nice Terry gentleman take look-see next side, see plenty nice box, you bet," he creaked.

"What's in those, Ramp Master?" Retief asked in tribal Voion, indicating the half-concealed boxes.

"Eee, the sir speaks good Tribal," the old Voion clacked

his palps in a gesture indicating Respectful Congratulation. "Why, as to those cases there, they contain educational material, yes, sir, that's what they contain. Now, over here . . ."

Big Leon had come up beside Retief. "Feel like sticking your nose into trouble?" Retief asked softly.

Leon nodded. "Sure, why not?"

"Why don't you go stir up a little activity over there, on the far side of the landing jack—say in about ten minutes?"

"Huh? Oh, I gotcha." Leon gave Retief a quizzical look, went over and spoke to Seymour. Beside Retief, the old Voion signaled with his antennae. A pair of cargo-handlers wheeled casually over to hover near the Terrans, trailing as they sauntered off, looking over the scene of bustling activity.

Retief moved on along the deep-shadowed lane between stacked cargo, paused before a heap of crates, pointed to the manila envelopes stapled to their sides.

"Mind if I look?" he inquired.

"As the sir desires," the oldster said quickly. Retief pulled a folded copy of a bill of lading from the pocket, opened it out. It indicated that the crate contained bound volumes of the *Pest Control Journal*, consigned to the Information Service Library in care of the Terran Consulate at Groon—a small city a hundred miles upriver in Deep Jungle. He went on, casually checking packing lists, rounded the end of the line of stacked crates, came up the back side. Directly behind the red-tagged cases, he found a pile of boxes, containing blank forms destined for the Terran Chancery. At that moment, an outcry came from beyond the looming bulk of the ship. Retief turned to his guide, who was now jittering nervously and looking in the direction from which the disturbance emanated.

"By the way, I forgot to mention it, but one of my companions—the large one—is something of a practical joker. He may have taken it into his head to start a fire or plant a couple of small choke-bombs. Maybe you'd better wheel over and check on him."

"The sir jests . . . ?" The Ramp Master looked around for a courier, saw the last of his crew curving sharply out of sight on one wheel, headed for the scene of the growing uproar. "If the sir will excuse . . ." he shot off at surprising speed.

At once, Retief turned to the nearest of the red-tagged crates, used a handy pry-bar to lever a slot free. A layer of oil-impregnated plastic barred his view of the contents of the box. He took out a compact pocket knife, snapped the blade out, slit the liner, reached in, felt a lumpy coolness of a plastic-coated object. He managed a two-fingered grip, drew it out. It was a bulky, heavy package, roughly triangular, larger than Retief's hand, its outlines obscured by the protective cocoon. He slit it, peeled it back; the polished butt of a Mark XXX power gun nestled in his hand.

Retief glanced around; none of the port personnel were in view. He stripped away the oily covering from the gun, dropped the weapon in his pocket, then tucked the empty plastic back inside, folded the liner over it, pressed the slat back in position.

The noises from Big Leon's direction were gaining in timbre and volume, accompanied by splintering sounds. Voom-Voom glanced at Retief. "Say, boss, that racket—"

"Just boyish high spirits; it won't last much longer," Retief said. "Meanwhile, see that nobody disturbs me for the next five minutes." Voom-Voom waved one arm, clicked his luminescent organ on, and rolled forward to cover the approach. Retief set to work moving the barricade of boxes aside and removing red tags from the special consignment. The riot continued, still growing in volume. With the tags free, Retief moved back to the crates marked for Groon, quickly removed the tags, used the butt of his pocket knife to hammer labels removed from the consignment of forms in place in their stead, then hurried on to the crated forms, placed the red tags on the boxes.

"Better hurry it up, boss," Voom-Voom hooted softly. "I think the excitement's dying down over there—" He broke off to rumble suddenly into action. Retief heard the shrill of Voion voices. He glanced up at the black disk of Joop; a glowing bulge was showing at one edge now; the eclipse would be over in another half-minute. He hurried back to the special consignment, attached the cards from the library shipment intended for Groon. Behind him, voices shrilled; Voom-Voom was still blocking the lane, loudly demanding why he should move merely to let a pack of Voion riffraff through. Retief stepped quickly to Rhum-Rhum.

"If you backed up carelessly, you might just ram that pile of boxes," he said. "They *might* get all mixed up together . . ."

"They might, at that," the Wumblum agreed. "Take those scalpers half their siesta hour to unscramble 'em." He straightened his wheels, glanced back, and moved suddenly, slammed into the neatly stacked crates. They skidded, toppled with a crash. Voom-Voom, watching the byplay with one pair of eyes, whirled about in mock alarm, dumped another row. Excited Voion shot past him, shrilling, just as the glare of returned sunlight sprang across the hills, scythed down the slope and on across the crowded tarmac to bathe the scene of chaos in brilliant day.

Big Leon appeared, looming over the scurrying cargo-tenders. He looked around, frowning.

"What the Sam Hill happened here?" he demanded loudly.

"Big brute of dumb Wumblum makee big mess-mess," the old Voion cargo master shrieked. "Great clumsy louts gotee no damn pidgin here!"

"Don't spin your wheels, grandpa," Voom-Voom rumbled carelessly. He leaned over to put his armored cranium near Retief's. "How'd I do, chief?"

"Very effective," Retief said approvingly. He walked over to the sidelines where a dull-eyed Vorch cargo-carrier was squatting, watching the activity.

"There are half a dozen crates marked for the Terry Library at Groon," he said in trade dialect to the heavyweight. "I wonder if you know of an unused shed nearby where they might accidentally be tucked away out of sight for a few days." He dropped a strip of embossed plastic trade wampum in the Vorch's nearest hand, which immediately twitched it out of sight.

"What's this—a bribe?" the carrier swiveled his wide head to bring his silicon-lensed rear eyes to bear.

"Just a gratuity for services rendered," Retief reassured him.

"That's OK then; just so you don't offer me no graft." The Vorch pointed with a short, thick arm. "The little

22

bonded warehouse over there—the one with the red carving on the front. I'll stack the stuff in there."

Retief nodded and rejoined the party.

"Hey, what gives, Mr. Retief?" Seymour demanded. "Leon says—"

"Maybe you better not ask too many questions," the big man put in. "I think we made our point. Let's settle for that and head back for Rum Jungle. Something's ready to pop, and I want to be minding the store when it happens."

"Maybe you better come with us, Retief," Steel-tooth said. "The post is a pretty fair fort if push comes to shove."

"Don't talk foolish, Lester," Leon said. "Retief's got a job to do here."

"Yeah," Steel-tooth said, "but when the job blows up in your face, remember Rum Jungle. We'll need every man—and then it won't be enough."

2

At the Terran Chancery in the Path of Many Sporting Agents, Retief stepped down from his perch and handed a strip of credit to his mount.

"Call on me any time, boss," the Wumblum said. "I kind of like your style." He nodded toward the irregularly surfaced Embassy complex, a cluster of standard Quopp-style buildings perched on the uneven ground, painted ocher, Indian red, and dusty aquamarine, perforated by irregularly shaped windows at random intervals. "First time I ever hauled a Terry," the Wumblum went on in a confidential tone. "Between you and me, I heard you folks were a tight crowd with a credit and not much in the sporting line, if you know what I mean."

"A base canard, Voom-Voom. A diplomat considers a day wasted if he isn't playing at least three games at once."

As Retief stepped through the main entry, incongruously aluminum-framed and glass-doored, First Secretary Magnan hurried up, a thin, harassed figure in the limp yellow seersucker shorts and dickey of subtropical undress kit.

"Retief," he called. "Wherever have you been? The

ambassador is furious! And Colonel Underknuckle's been calling for you for an hour! I've been frantic!"

"Why? Can't they be furious without me?"

"The sight of you seems to stimulate the condition, that I grant," Magnan said witheringly. "Come along now. I've told the colonel you were probably out gathering material for the quarterly Sewage Report. I trust you'll say nothing to dispel that impression."

"I've been cementing relations with the Terran business community," Retief explained as he accompanied the senior diplomat along the wide, tiled, office-lined corridor which had been installed to replace the warren of tiny, twisting passages and cubicles originally filling the interior of the structure.

"Hmmm. I'm not sure that was wise, in view of the present down-playing of Terran private enterprise here on Quopp. You know how Prime Minister Ikk frowns on that sort of thing."

"Oh, prime minister, eh? Who gave him that title?"

"Why, he advised the ambassador that it was conferred early this morning by unanimous vote of the Council of Drones." Retief followed Magnan into the lift; the doors closed with a soft *whoosh!* of compressed air. The car lurched, started heavily upward.

"Let's see," Retief mused. "That's the dummy legislature he set up to satisfy the ambassador's passion for democracy, isn't it? It was fortunate he had seventy-three senile uncles handy to appoint; saved the bother of breaking in strangers."

"Yours is a distorted view of the evolution of representational government here on Quopp," Magnan said reprovingly. "Closer attention to your *Daily Bulletin from the Bird's Nest* would go far toward homogenizing your thinking on the subject."

"I thought that was something they did to milk."

"The term refers to voluntary alignment of viewpoint toward a group-oriented polarity; a sort of linkage of moral horsepower for maximal thrust toward the objective."

"I'm not sure that pasteurized thinking is rich enough in intellectual vitamins to satisfy my growing curiosity about just what Ikk is up to."

"It should be apparent even to you, Retief," Magnan

said sharply, "that the Corps can hardly accredit a full Mission to a nonexistent planetary government. Ergo, such a ruling body must be formed—and who better qualified than the Voion to undertake the task?"

"You might have something there; their past history has given them a firm grounding in the basics of politics; but with the other tribes outnumbering them a hundred to one, it's a little hard to see how they're planning to impose planet-wide enlightenment on a race that's as fond of anarchy as the Quoppina."

"That, my dear Retief, is Ambassador Longspoon's problem, not ours. It was his idea to groom the Voion for leadership; our task is merely to implement his policies."

"And if in the process we saddle the other ninety-nine percent of the population with a dictatorship, that's a mere detail."

"Ah, I can see you're beginning to get the picture. Now . . ." The elevator halted and Magnan led the way out, paused at the heavy door barring the public from the Chancery wing. "I hope you'll restrain your unfortunate tendency to essay japes at the expense of decorum, Retief. Colonel Underknuckle is in no mood for facetiae." He pushed through, nodded mechanically at the small, gray Voion female buffing her chelae at a small desk of polished blue wood at one side of the red-carpeted corridor. She clacked her palps indifferently, blew a large bubble of green spearmint, and popped it with lively report.

"Impertinence!" Magnan sniffed under his breath. "A few months ago the baggage was an apprentice slop-drudge in a local inn of most unsavory repute; now, after we've trained her and given her that expensive set of chrome inlays, a derisive pop of the gum is considered adequate greeting for her benefactors."

"That's the trouble with uplifting the masses; they get to believing it themselves."

Magnan stopped at an austere slab door marked MILITARY ATTACHE, fitted an expression on his narrow features appropriate for greeting a Grade Seven employee, pushed through into deep-carpeted silence.

"Ah, there, Hernia, I believe Colonel Underknuckle wished to see Mr. Retief . . ."

The fat woman behind the desk patted a coil of mummified hair with a hand like a glove full of lard, showed

Magnan a simper suitable for a first secretary, thumbed a button on a console before her. A chime sounded beyond the half-open door.

"Yes, confound it, what is it this time!" a voice like splitting canvas snarled from the desk speaker. "What in the name of perdition's become of Magnan? If he's not here in five minutes, send along that memo to the ambassador I keep handy—"

"It is I," Magnan said stiffly. "And—"

"Don't use grammar on me, Magnan!" the attaché shouted. "Come in here at once! There's been another communication from that benighted vessel! The saucy minx at the controls insists she's bringing her in, clearance or no clearance. And where the devil's that fellow, Retief?"

"I have him right here, Colonel . . ." As his callers entered the room, Underknuckle, a lean, high-shouldered man with bushy white hair, hollow, purplish cheeks, and a lumpy, clay-colored nose, his immaculately tailored midafternoon semiformal uniform awry, spun in his hip-u-matic contour chair, causing the power-swivel mechanism to whine in protest. He glared at Retief.

"So there you are at last! What's the meaning of this, sir? Is it possible that you're unaware of the new restrictions on tourism here on Quopp?" The colonel lowered his voice. "Schemes are all about us, gentlemen. We'll have to look sharp to our fences to keep our powder dry!"

"But just one little shipload of ladies—and in difficulty at that—" Magnan began.

"Orders are orders!" Underknuckle hit the desk with his fist, winced, slung his fingers as though drying them.

"Let me assure you, when Ambassador Longspoon imposed entry quotas on sightseers, there was an excellent reason for it!" He barked through a grimace of pain.

"Gracious, yes, Colonel," Magnan chirped. "We all know Prime Minister Ikk doesn't like Terries."

"Ikk's likes and dislikes have nothing to do with it! It was the ambassador's decision!"

"Of course, Colonel. What I meant was, you don't like Terries—"

"Don't like Terrans? Why, I'm a Terran myself, you idiot!"

"I didn't mean to give the wrong impression, I'm sure,

Fred," Magnan said breathlessly. "Personally, I *love* Terries—"

"Not *these* Terries!" Underknuckle snatched up a paper and waved it. "A boatload of females! Giddy, irresponsible, women! Idlers—or worse! Parasites! And no visas, mind you! And the ringleader, Mr. Retief"—the colonel thrust a mobile lower lip at him—"is demanding to speak to *you*, sir! By name!"

"Retief!" Magnan turned on him. "What can you be thinking of, importing luxury goods—"

"It's clear enough what he's thinking of," Underknuckle snapped. "And I needn't point out that such thoughts are hardly in consonance with tight military security!"

Magnan assumed a troubled-but-determined expression. "Did the young lady give a name?"

"Harrumph! Indeed she did. 'Tell him it's Fifi,' she said—as though the military attaché were a common messenger boy!"

"Heavens—such cheek!" Magnan sniffed.

"The name itself conjures up images of rhinestone-clad doxies," Underknuckle snorted. "I confess it's difficult to understand how a diplomat has occasion to make the acquaintance of persons of such stripe!"

"Oh, I'm sure Mr. Retief can fix you up, Fred," Magnan volunteered. "He seems to have a knack—"

"I do not wish to be fixed up!" Underknuckle roared. "I wish to make it clear to these junketing trollops that they will not be permitted to make planetfall here! Now, if you, Mr. Retief, will be so kind as to report to the Message Center and so inform your, ah, *petite amie*—"

"I don't have an *amie* at the moment, Colonel, *petite* or otherwise," Retief said. "And, as it happens, I don't know any young ladies named Fifi. Still, it's never too late to rectify the omission. I'll be happy to talk to her."

"I'm gratified to hear it," Underknuckle said coldly. "And if that vessel lands on this planet, young man, I'll hold you solely responsible!"

Back in the corridor, Magnan trotted at Retief's side, offering advice. "Now, just tell this young person, kindly but firmly, that your time is fully occupied by your duties and that if she'll just flit along to Adobe, say—there's a fascinating museum there with a lovely display of mummified giant spiders—"

"I won't presume to plan any itineraries," Retief interrupted gently. "I think it might be better to find out what the girls are up to, first."

"Yes, it does seem odd they'd plan a vacation on Quopp; after all, there's nothing here but jungle, with a few thousand tribal villages and three or four dozen market towns."

They turned in at the Message Center, showed badges; electro-locks clicked and the inner door slid back, revealing a bright-lit room crammed with lock-files and coding machines.

"Oh boy, am I glad to see you, Mr. Retief," a freckled youth with thick contact lenses and a struggling moustache blurted, coming forward. "That babe aboard the yacht's a dish, all right, but she's got a way of flashing her eyes at a fellow when she doesn't get her way—"

"If you don't mind, Willis, Mr. Retief and I are in something of a hurry," Magnan cut him off. "Which screen are they on?"

"The yacht's over the horizon at the moment," the boy said. "She'll make reentry on the next pass; a couple more minutes, I guess."

"What's a yacht doing out here, Willy?" Retief asked. "Quopp's a long way off the regular tourist runs."

"Beats me, Mr. Retief. She's a nice job—ten thousand tons, loaded with all the latest comm gear. Too bad all we have is this obsolete line-of-sight stuff." He gestured at the banked equipment panels. "Tough about those girls losing their celestial tracking circuit, too. Even if they could get in here, they'd be stuck for months waiting for a replacement. That Mark XXXIV stuff is hard to come by."

"Emergency letdown, eh? What kind of help are we giving them?"

The youth shrugged, "None-Longspoon's orders. Says they've got no business coming in on Quopp."

"Did you tell him about the tracker?"

"He said they could go on to the next system on manual tracking—"

"Two months of staring into a tracker scope could get tiring," Retief said. "And a good chance of fatigue error and no planet-fall at the end of it. Let's get 'em down."

"Yeah, but the ambassador's orders—"

"I'll take the responsibility of countermanding them. Get the yacht on the SDR and start feeding her data as soon as she makes contact again."

"Look here, Retief," Magnan held up an admonitory hand. "I can't stand idly by while you exceed your authority! I confess it seems a trifle surprising the ambassador hasn't authorized aid to a distressed Terran vessel, but—"

"We don't need authorization in a Deep Space emergency. Check Title Nine, Article Twelve, Section three-B of the Uniform Code."

"Hey, that's right," Willis blinked. "The code overrides any planetary authority, it says so right in—"

"See here, Retief," Magnan moved to Retief's side, speaking low. "Quoting technicalities is all very well, but afterward one still has the problem of an overriden ambassador to deal with. Hardly a shrewd move, career-wise . . ."

"We'll get the ladies down first, and carry out career salvage afterward," Retief said soothingly. "Maybe it would be better if you went down to spot-check the commissary while I attend to this."

Magnan frowned, settled his dickey in place. "Never mind," he said shortly. "I'll stand by."

A blare of static burst from the center screen on the console across the room, followed by rapidly flickering bars of light; then the image steadied into focus. A girl's face appeared, framed in red-blond hair, a headset clamped in place. Other feminine faces were visible behind her, all young, all worried.

"Hello, Quopp Control," she said calmly. "It looks as though the rock that hulled us did more than take out the tracker. I have no horizontal gyros, and damned little control in my left corrector banks. I'm going to have to do this by the seat-of-the-pants method. I'd appreciate it if you'd loosen up and feed me some trajectory data."

Retief flipped the SEND key.

"Quopp Control here, young lady. Listen closely; there won't be time for a repeat. You have two choices on impact areas; one is the commercial port here at Ixix. If you've got a fix on me, you know the general location. I'm throwing the R and D fixer beam on the line now; lock into it if you can—"

The girl frowned. "Sorry, Quopp Control. No response from my R and D. I have a fix on your transmission, though, and—"

"Your other possibility is an unimproved patch of rocky desert about fifty miles north-north-west. Try to align on my signal here; if you miss, you'll have the other as a backup."

"Roger, Quopp Tower. I've got some speed to kill if I want to make you on this pass—"

"This pass is it," Retief rapped out. "I'm clocking you on a descending spiral with an intersect this orbit. Damp that velocity fast!"

The image on the screen jittered and jumped; Retief waited while the girl worked the controls, watching the glowing red blip moving rapidly across the R and D screen, dropping steadily closer to the line representing the horizon.

"More grief," the girl said briskly. "I've got about half power on the forward main tubes. I'm afraid I'm going to have to give your beacon a miss and try for the desert."

"Throw everything you've got to your retros, let 'em blast and keep blasting! You're going to overshoot by a hundred miles on your present course, and there's nothing out there but nineteen thousand miles of unexplored jungle!"

There was a long moment of tense silence as the girl's hands moved out of sight. Then she shook her head, gave a quick, flashing smile. "That's it, Quopp Control. A fizzle. Did you say nineteen thousand miles?"

"As the Phip flies. How many are there aboard?"

"Ten of us."

"I've got a tracker on you; try to nurse her in as easy as you can. Got any flares aboard?"

"If not, there are a few cases of hundred and sixty proof Imperial Lily gin; I'm sure the intended recipient won't mind if I light them off." Already, her voice was growing fuzzy as the hurtling ship neared the horizon.

"Hold her steady on your present course. Looks like you'll intersect ground zero about eighty miles out."

"I'm not reading you, Quopp. I hope you get here before all the gin's—" Her voice broke off. Then it came again, faint and far away: "Quopp . . . er, a . . . ing in . . . make it . . ." The voice was gone in a rising hiss of random noise.

"Good Lord, I hope the poor girls land safely," Magnan gasped; he dabbed at his forehead with a large floral-patterned tissue. "Imagine being down in that horrible wilderness, swarming with unpacified Quoppina—"

"I'll get an Embassy heli on the way to make the pickup," Retief said; he glanced at the wall clock. "No time to waste if we're going to collect them by dark."

"Retief—are you *sure* you don't know this Fifi person?" Magnan queried as they turned to the door.

"Regrettably, no. But I hope to correct the omission soon—"

The interoffice communicator screen burped; an angular female face with stiff-looking hair and a porridgy complexion blinked into focus.

"There you are," she snapped at Retief. "The ambassador wants to see you in his office—right away!"

"Tsk," Magnan said. "I warned you about stretching those coffee breaks . . ."

"Hi, Fester," Retief greeted the woman. "Is it business, or should I bring my tennis racket?"

"You can save the wisecracks," she sniffed. "There are two Planetary Police officers with him."

"Goodness, I'd be glad to give His Excellency a character reference," Magnan burbled. "What did they catch —that is, what's the charge?"

"It's not Ambassador Longspoon who's in trouble," Fester said coldly. "It's Mr. Retief they want to see."

Ambassador Longspoon was a small man with bright, close-set eyes in a parchment-yellow face, a mouth which would have been inconspicuous on a carp, and a shiny skull over which a few strands of damp-looking hair were combed for maximum coverage. He sat behind a nine-foot ambassadorial desk of polished platinum, flanked by two Voion, one ornately crested and jeweled, whose oculars followed Retief unwaveringly as he entered the room.

"Commissioner Ziz, Mr. Retief," Longspoon said in a voice like a dry bearing. There was silence as he looked expectantly from one of the Voion to the other.

"Well, how about it, Xif," the commissioner buzzed in harsh tribal Voion to his companion. "Is this the one?"

"That's him, chief," the other cop confirmed. "He was the ringleader."

"Here, Commissioner, I must ask you to speak Terran!" Longspoon rasped.

"Just advising my associate that he mustn't harbor grudges for the brutal treatment he received," Ziz said smoothly. "I assured him Your Excellency will make full amends."

"Amends. Yes." Longspoon favored Retief with a look like a jab from an old maid's umbrella. "It appears there's been some sort of free-for-all in an unsavory local drinking spot." He put bony fingers on the desk top and pinched them together. "I trust you have some explanation?"

"Explanation of what, Mr. Ambassador?" Retief inquired pleasantly.

"Of just what would possess an Embassy Officer to attack members of the Planetary Police in the performance of their duties!" Purplish color was creeping up from under Longspoon's stiff midmorning informal collar.

Retief shook his head sympathetically. "No, I certainly couldn't explain a thing like that."

Longspoon's lower jaw dropped. "Surely you have *some*, ah, justification to offer?" He shot a quick side glance at the Voion.

"It would be pretty hard to justify attacking a policeman," Retief offered. "In the performance of his duties at that."

"Look here . . . !" Longspoon leaned toward Retief. "You're supposed to be a diplomat!" he hissed from the corner of his mouth. "You might at least try lying a little!"

Retief nodded agreeably. "What about?"

"Confound it, sir!" Longspoon waved a hand. "When a police commissioner rolls into my office and charges one of my staff with aggravated breach of the peace, you can hardly expect me to simply ignore the situation!"

"Certainly not," Retief said firmly. "Still I think if you explain to him that invading the Terrestrial Embassy to make unsupported charges is impolite, and warn him never to try it again, it won't be necessary to demand his resignation—"

"His resignation!" Longspoon's mouth was open again.

"Hmmm . . ." He swiveled to face the commissioner. "Perhaps I should point out that invading the Terrestrial Embassy to make unsup—"

"One moment!" Ziz cut in harshly. "The question here is one of appropriate punishment to lawless foreigners who engage in the murder of harmless, grub-loving Voion! I demand that the culprit be turned over to me for a fair Trial by Internal Omens!"

"As I recall, the method requires a surgical operation to study the evidence," Longspoon mused. "What happens if the victim, er, I mean patient, is innocent?"

"Then we weld him back up and give him a touching funeral ceremony."

"No, Ziz," Longspoon wagged a finger playfully. "If we simply turned our diplomats over to anyone who wanted them, we'd be stripped of personnel in no time."

"Just the one," Ziz suggested delicately.

"I'd like to oblige, my dear Commissioner, but the precedent would be most unfortunate."

The desk screen chimed apologetically.

"Yes, Fester?" Longspoon eyed it impatiently. "I told you I wasn't to be disturbed—"

"It's His Omnivoracity," Fester squeaked excitedly. "He presents his second best compliments and insists on speaking to you at once, Mr. Ambassador!"

Longspoon twitched a bleak smile at the police commissioner. "Well, my good friend Ikk seems to be a bit outside himself today. Just tell him I'll ring him up later, Fester—"

"He says it's about an educational shipment," the female cut in. "Heavens, what language!"

"Ah, yes, educational material," Longspoon said. "Well, I'm always most concerned about educational affairs; perhaps I'd best just see what he has in mind . . ." He turned the volume down low, listened as a tiny voice chirped angrily.

"Are you sure?" he muttered. "Six cases?"

There was more shrill talk from the communicator.

"Nonsense!" Longspoon snapped. "What possible motive—"

Ikk buzzed again. Longspoon glanced at Retief with a startled expression. "No," he said. "Quite out of the question. See here, I'll call you back. I have, er, callers at the moment." He rang off. The police commissioner relaxed the auditory members which had been straining forward during the exchange.

"You still refuse to remand this one to my custody?" He pointed at Retief.

"Have you all gone mad?" Longspoon barked. "I'll deal with Mr. Retief in my own way—"

"In that case . . ." Ziz turned to his retainer. "Put phase two into operation," he snapped in Tribal. "Just sending the lad along to water the jelly flowers down at headquarters," he added soothingly as Longspoon drew breath to protest. Xif wheeled across to the door, left silently. Ziz rolled to the lopsidedly hexagonal window, glanced out into the street.

"A pity Your Excellency didn't see fit to assist the police in the maintenance of law and order," he said, turning to Longspoon. "However, I shall take the disappointment philosophically . . ." He broke off, waving both posterior antennae. "Hark!" he said. "Do I scent a suspicious odor!"

Longspoon cleared his throat hurriedly. "My throat balm," he said. "My physician insists . . ." He sniffed again. "Smoke!" He jumped to his feet. At that moment, a shrill bell jangled into strident life somewhere beyond the door.

"Flee for your lives!" Ziz keened. He shot to the door, flung it wide. A billow of black smoke bulged into the room. Longspoon dithered for a moment, then grabbed up a code book and the Classified Despatch reel, tossed them into his desk-side safe, slammed it shut just as a pair of Voion charged into the room, hauling a heavy fire hose with a massive brass nozzle from which a weak stream of muddy water dribbled into the deep-pile carpeting. Ziz barked a command and pointed at Retief; the firemen dropped the hose—and were bowled aside as Ambassador Longspoon hurtled between them, his basketball-sized paunch jouncing under overlapping vests. Ziz spun, reached for Retief with a pair of horny grasping members; the Terran leaned aside, caught one of the Voion's arms and jerked; Ziz went over with a crash.

Retief whirled to the window from which the commissioner had glanced a moment before, saw a crowd of crested and ornamented Voion police pressing toward the Embassy doors.

"Fast action," he murmured. He stepped past the over-turned firemen into the corridor; wide-eyed staff members were appearing from doors, batting at smoke clouds. Shouts and squeals sounded. Retief pushed through to-ward an open door from which dense yellowish clouds were pouring, layering out at chest height. He reached the far wall of the room, groped for and found an overturned typist's chair, slammed it at the dim glow of a small tri-angular window. The colored glass fell outward with a musical tinkle. At once, the smoke—boiling from an over-turned wastebasket, Retief saw—was swept toward the opening by a strong draft. He picked up the smoking wastebasket and contents, stepped into the lavatory and doused it with water; it died with a prolonged hiss. Retief lifted a small, soot-blackened plastic canister from the bas-ket; a small wisp of smoke was still coiling from it; incised on its base were what appeared to be Groaci hieroglyphs.

Back in the hall, First Secretary Magnan appeared from a smoke cloud, coughing, eyes blurred.

"Retief! The service door's jammed with people! We're trapped!"

"Let's try another route." Retief started toward the front of the building, Magnan trailing.

"But—what about the others!"

"I predict the fire scare will give them excellent appe-tites for dinner."

"Scare?"

"It seems to be just smoke bombs."

"You mean—Retief! You didn't—"

"No, but somebody did." They reached the wide hall before the main Embassy entrance door, packed now with excited diplomats and semihysterical stenographers milling in the smoke, and swarms of Voion firemen, wheeling au-thoritatively through the press, shrilling the alarm. More Voion were struggling in the door to breast the tide of escape-bent Terrans.

"All personnel must evacuate the premises at once," a cop with a bright red inlay across his ventral plates keened. "Collapse is imminent! The danger is frightful! Remember, you are all highly combustible . . . !"

"I don't know what the game is, but we'd better have a

fast look around." Retief headed for a side corridor. A stout diplomat with four boneless chins flapped a hand at him.

"I say, young man, all these locals invading the Terrestrial Embassy—it's irregular! Now, I want you to speak to Chief Sskt, and point out—"

"Sorry, Counselor Eggwalk; rush job." Retief pushed past, forced his way through a shouting knot of entangled police and Terrans, rounded a curve in the corridor. A small door marked MAINTENANCE PERSONNEL ONLY caught his eye. It stood ajar; the lock, Retief noted, was broken.

"Mr. Magnan, if you see any volunteer firemen headed this way, give me a fast yell."

"Retief! What are you—"

Magnan's voice cut off as Retief slid through the door, went down a narrow ramp into the cool of a low-ceilinged cellar. There was a scurry of sound ahead; he ducked under insulated air ducts, saw a flicker of motion down a shadowy passage, heard the scrape of wheels scuffling on uneven pavement.

"Come on out," he called. "Nothing back there but a couple of sump pumps and some bilge water."

The sounds had ceased now. Retief took a step—and a three-foot yellow-green Quoppina of the Dink tribe shot out of the darkness, ducked under his arm, veered around the looming bulk of the furnace, disappeared into the dark mouth of a narrow crawlway. Retief paused, listening. There was a soft buzzing from far back in the recess where the Dink had hidden. He ducked his head, moved toward the source of the sound. Above, the thudding of feet and the shouts of Terran and Voion were faint, remote. Somewhere, water dripped.

Retief followed the sound, traced it to a dark crevice behind the metal-clad housing of an air-processing unit. He reached in, brought out a foot-long ovoid, plastic-surfaced. It hummed busily; he could feel the tiny vibration against his hands. He spun, headed for the ramp.

Back in the hall, Magnan was nowhere in sight. Ten feet away, a Voion cop stood on relaxed, outward-slanting wheels, talking into a small field microphone. He broke off when he saw Retief, jerked two arms in a commanding gesture.

"Out! Fire has reached boilers!" he rasped in badly accented trade dialect.

Retief balanced the humming object on one outstretched hand. "You know what this is?" he inquired casually.

"No time for ball games," the Voion shrilled. "Fool Terry—" He stopped, snapped his anterior eyes forward, made a whistling noise between his palps, then spun, dug off with a squeak of new Terry-issue neoprene. Retief turned toward a side exit. Two Voion appeared ahead, skidded to a halt at sight of him.

"That's him!" one shrilled. "Get him, boys!" More Voion shot into view, closing in. "Don't move, stilter!" the cop commanded. "What's that you're holding?"

"This?" Retief juggled the ovoid. "Oh, this is just an old Plooch egg. I was just cleaning out my collection, and—"

"You lie, unwheeled crippling!" The cops crowded in reaching. "I'll wager a liter of Hellrose it's part of the loot!" one keened. "It'll mean promotions all around when we bring *this* in!"

"Give me that, you!" eager Voion manipulative members grabbed for the buzzing object. "We'll take it out the back way!"

"Sure, you have it, fellows," Retief offered genially. "Just hurry back to your boss with it—"

"Bribes will do you no good, Terran," a cop shrilled as the find was passed from one gleeful fireman to another. "His Omnivoracity wants to see you—in person." He jabbed with his club at Retief, who caught the heavy weapon, jerked it from its owner's grip, slammed it across his wrist with a metallic clang. More clubs flashed; Retief fended off blows, then charged, slamming Voion in all directions. A club whistled past his ear; a harsh voice shrilled, "Stop him!" Ahead, a dim blue light glowed over a side door. Retief skidded to a halt, tried it: locked. He stepped back, kicked at the lock; the door burst wide. Retief plunged through into a narrow street—and stopped dead facing a solid rank of Voion who ringed him in with leveled spears featuring prominently barbed heads.

"Welcome to our midst," a police lieutenant with an enameled badge hissed. "You will now accompany us without resistance, or you will die, unseen by your fellows."

"Ah-ah," Retief chided. "Ikk will be annoyed if you do anything rash."

"An excellent point," the cop agreed. "I suppose after all we shall have to satisfy ourselves with merely poking holes in you here and there. The effect will be the same."

"Your logic is inescapable," Retief conceded. "I'll be delighted to call on His Omnivoracity."

There was a sharp tremor underfoot, followed instantly by a dull Boom! and a shower of plaster dust from the open door at Retief's back. Glass tinkled, falling from nearby windows. Shrill Voion sounds broke out, questioning. Retief turned, surveyed the wall of the Embassy tower. A large crack had appeared some yards to the right of the door.

"I guess it wasn't a Plooch egg after all," he said judiciously.

The spearheads had jumped a foot closer at the explosion. "Watch him!" the lieutenant barked.

"Steady, boys," Retief cautioned. "Don't louse up an important pinch with any hasty moves."

"Button your mandibles," the cop rasped. "You'll have your chance to work them soon enough!" He motioned and an avenue opened through the warriors. Retief moved off, spear-points at his back.

3

Prime Minister Ikk was a larger than average Voion with a sixteen-coat lacquer job, jeweled palps, and an elaborately crested headpiece featuring metallic turquoise curlicues and white Rhoon plumes. He lounged at ease in his office, a wide, garishly decorated room the floor of which, Retief noted, was scattered with blank CDT forms. The Voion's main wheels were braced in padded, satin-lined frames; a peculiarly vile-smelling dope-stick of Groaci manufacture was clamped in one manipulative member. He waved the latter at the guards standing by, dribbling ashes carelessly on the rug.

"Leave us," he snapped in Tribal. "And no spying, either!" The cops filed out silently. Ikk waited until the door closed, then swiveled to stare at Retief.

"So, you are the person." He canted both sets of antennae forward alertly. "It seems we had a busy morning, eh?" His voice had an edge like torn metal.

"Rather dull, actually," Retief said easily. "Sight-seeing, you know."

"And what sort of sights did you see . . . ?"

"Some rather interesting examples of Navajo beadwork

and a nice display of hand-painted Groaci back-scratchers. Then there was—"

"Save your flippancy, Terran!" Ikk snapped. "Your activities are known! It remains merely to fill in certain, ah, details!"

"Perhaps you'd care to be a little more specific," Retief suggested. "After all, nobody's listening."

"You were seen at the port," Ikk grated. "You created a disturbance, after which certain items were found to be missing."

"Oh? What items?"

"Six large cases, newly arrived aboard a chartered freight vessel," Ikk snapped. "They contained educational material destined to play an important role in my program for the uplift of the downtrodden Quoppina masses."

"I see; and you think I may have picked them up and strolled off without noticing."

"An end to your insolence," Ikk snarled. "What have you done with the purloined consignment?"

Retief shook his head. "I haven't seen your school books, Mr. Prime Minister."

"Bah; enough of this verbal pussyfooting! You know what the cases contain as well as I—"

"I believe you mentioned educational material—"

"What could be more educational than guns?" Ikk screeched. "The truth, now!"

"The truth is, you're making a blunder, Ikk. Your fellow Quoppina aren't as ready for compulsory education as you seem to imagine."

"If they've grown wise at my expense—through *your* meddling," Ikk cut in, "I promise you an enlightening experience under the implements of a staff of experienced speech tutors!"

"I'm sure your training aids are tucked safely away out of circulation," Retief said soothingly. "That being the case, I suggest you reappraise the whole indoctrination program and try a less ambitious approach."

"Ah, I see it now!" Ikk shrilled. "Longspoon thinks to unseat me, replace me with some compliant puppet—a Herpp, perhaps, or one of those wishy-washy Yerkle! Well, it won't work!" He lowered his voice suddenly. "See here, my good fellow, I'm sure we could work out something. Just tell me where you've hidden the guns and I'll see to it you're appropriately rewarded after the enlightenment."

"That's a fascinating proposal, Mr. Prime Minister. But I'm afraid I'd lie awake nights wondering what you considered appropriate. No, on the whole I think I'd prefer to take my chances on my own."

"An opportunity you are hardly likely to enjoy," Ikk grated, "considering the fact that I have fifty thousand crack troops in the city at this moment, all of them between you and your friends."

"Fifty thousand, you say," Retief countered. "That's not a big enough army for a first class victory parade, to say nothing of taking over a planet with a population of five billion argumentative Quoppina."

"The fifty thousand I mentioned are merely my household detachment," Ikk purred. "Every Voion on Quopp answers to me—two million of them! They've been training for a year at secret camps in the Deep Jungle. They are now ready!"

"Except for the guns," Retief said. "Still, there were only a few hundred of them; they wouldn't have helped you much—"

"Today's shipment was but the first of many! But enough of this gossip! For the last time: Give up your secret and enjoy my lasting favor!"

"You mean if I tell you, you'll give me an escort back to the Embassy, no hard feelings?"

"Certainly, my dear chap! I'll even concoct a stirring tale of your abduction by unscrupulous elements from whom I effected your rescue, not neglecting to mention your own brisk resistance to their wiles."

"Brisker than you anticipated, perhaps," Retief said. "I think I've learned enough to satisfy my curiosity, so—if you'll just move away from that desk and back up against the wall . . ."

Ikk erected his oculars violently. "Eh—" He broke off, looking at the gleaming new power gun in Retief's hand.

"What's this?" he squeaked. "I've offered you safe conduct . . . !"

"Now, Ikk, you don't really think I'd expect a campaigner of your experience to let me off scot-free, do you?"

"Well, my fellows might have to employ just a few little measures on you to be sure you weren't holding anything back—but then I'll have them patch you up nicely afterward."

"Sorry—but I have a strong intuitive feeling that your Torture Department may not realize just how fragile human hide is."

"I shall know in a moment." The prime minister started toward Retief—six feet of armored hostility, four arms like sheet-metal clubs tipped with bolt-cutters cocked for action.

"I can see that Your Omnivoracity hasn't yet sampled Terran educational methods personally," Retief commented. "Another foot and I'll give you your first lesson."

Ikk halted. "Would you dare?" He keened.

"Sure. Why not? Now, don't make any sudden moves. I'm going to tie you up. Then I'm leaving."

Ikk hissed but submitted as Retief plucked the ministerial flag from its place, thrust the staff through his spokes and bound it in place, then tied all four arms firmly.

"There, now, you'll be all right until the sweepers arrive along about dinner time."

"You're a fool!" Ikk shrilled. "You'll never get clear of the building!"

"Perhaps not," Retief said. "In that case, education may never come to Quopp." He went to the intercom. "When I flip the key, tell them I'm coming out," he said. "Tell them to trail me at a respectful distance, because I'm suspicious. Also, you're not to be disturbed until further notice. Sound like you mean it."

Ikk clacked his palps.

"And," Retief added in fluent Voion thieves' dialect, "don't make any mistakes." He pressed the key.

"What is it this time?" a sharp Voion voice came back. Retief held the gun aimed at Ikk's center ventral plate while the prime minister delivered the message.

"Well done, Ikk." Retief flipped off the switch, bent it out of line to render it inoperative. "You may yell all you like now; I have great confidence in ministerial soundproofing."

"Listen to me, Terry!" Ikk keened. "Give up this madness! My troops will hunt you down without mercy! And what can you hope to accomplish alone?"

"Ah, that's the question, isn't it, Ikk?" Retief went to the door. "And on that note I'll leave you. . . ."

43

In the outer office the bodyguards standing by swiveled their oculars nervously at Retief.

"Ikk's tied up for the rest of the afternoon," he said breezily. "He's busy pondering some surprising new developments." He stepped into the corridor, made his way along narrow, strange-smelling passages, winding, dipping, curiously angled, lit by chemical lamps and lined with cubicles from which bright Voion eyes glinted. He emerged in a cramped courtyard surrounded by high, curving, decoration-crusted walls of faded Burgundy and Prussian blue, gleaming in the eerie light of Second Eclipse. There were, if anything, more police gathered now than an hour before. A ripple seemed to pass across the crowd as Retief appeared—twitching antennae semaphoring a message. At once, a path opened through the press.

In the open street the mob was scarcely less dense. Voion—both polished police and dull-finished tribesmen —stood in rows, packed the parking ledges, jostled for wheel-space in the narrow thoroughfare. Here and there a tall bottle-green Yerkle or blue-and-white Clute hurried, a furtive touch of color against the sea of restless black. Through lighted shop windows, Quoppina of other tribes were visible, gathered in tight groups, watching the street. Except for a steady, subdued buzzing in the Voion dialects, the city was ominously silent.

Retief strode along briskly, the Voion continuing to inobtrusively edge from his path. On a street corner he paused, glanced back. A pair of crested Special Police were shouldering through, keeping a fifty-foot interval between themselves and the object of the prime minister's instructions. A third Voion came up behind them, shrilled a command. The two came on at a quick roll. Retief pushed on across the street, turned down a narrow sideway. Ahead, there was a stir. More of the tall Special Police appeared, keening orders to those about them. A message rippled across the crowd. To the right, three more cops had come into view, pushing through toward him, clubs prominently displayed.

"Maybe you'd better step in to avoid the crowd, Terry," a thing voice said at Retief's back. He turned. A small, purplish, lightly built Quopp of the Flink tribe stood in the doorway of a tiny shop. He stepped back; Retief

44

followed, glanced around at shelves loaded with trinkets; Yalcan glasswork, Jaq beaten copper-ware, wooden objects from far-off Lovenbroy, a dim-lit display of Hoogan religious mosaics featuring the Twelve Ritual Dismemberments.

"That one caught your eye, didn't it?" the Flink said. "That's always been a snappy seller with you Terries."

"It's a winner," Retief agreed. "There wouldn't be a back way out of here, I suppose?"

The Flink was staring out at the street. "Ikk's up to something big this time; such a force he never had in town before. Half his tribe he's got in the streets, just standing around like it was a signal they was waiting for." He turned to look at Retief. "Yep, there's a back way—but you won't get far; not if Ikk's bully boys are looking for you. Right now, you must be the only Terry in Ixix still running around loose."

"That's a distinction I'd like to retain," Retief pointed out.

"Terry, I'd like to help you out," the Flink waggled his head. "But you're as easy to spot as an off-color grub at a hatching ceremony—" He broke off, twitched vestigial wing cases, producing a sharp pop. "Unless . . ." he said. "Terry, are you game to try something risky?"

"It couldn't be any riskier than standing here," Retief said. "The cops are closing in from all four directions."

"Come on." The Flink flipped aside a hanging, waved Retief through into an even tinier chamber behind the shop, from which a number of dark tunnel-mouths opened —mere holes, two feet in diameter.

"You'll have to crawl, I'm afraid," he said.

"One of the basic diplomatic skills," Retief said. "Lead on."

It was a five-minute trip through the cramped passage, which twisted and writhed, doubled back, rose suddenly, then dropped, did a sharp jag to the left, and opened into a leather-and-wax smelling chamber, lit by a sour-yellow chemical lamp inside a glass bowl. The room was stacked with curiously shaped objects of all sizes and colors. Retief snapped a finger against the nearest—a large, shield-shaped panel of a shimmering pearly pink. It gave off a metallic bong.

"These look like fragments of native anatomy," he said.

"Right. This is the back room of Sopp's Surgical Spares; Sopp has the best stock in the district. Come on."

Hobbling on small wheels better adapted to trolley service than ground-running, the Flink led the way past heaped carapace segments of glossy chocolate brown, screaming orange, butter-yellow, chartreuse, magenta, coppery red. Some of the metallo-chitinous plates bore ribs, bosses, knobs, spikes; some were varicolored, with polka dots and ribbons of contrasting color, or elaborate silver-edged rosettes. A few bore feathers, scales or bristles. At one side were ranged bins filled with gears, bearings, shafts, electronic components.

"Yep, for anything in the used parts line, old Sopp's the Quopp to see," the Flink said. "He can pull this off if anybody can. Wait here a minute." He stepped through an arched opening into the display room beyond.

"Hey, Sopp, close the blinds," Retief heard him say. "I've got a friend with me that doesn't want to attract any attention . . ." There was an answering twitter, a clatter of wooden shutters, followed by more low-voiced conversation punctuated with exclamations from the unseen proprietor. Then the Flink called. Retief came through into a neat showroom with cases filled with bright-colored objects of obscure function, presided over by a frail-looking Yerkle with a deep green carapace half-concealed under a silken paisley-patterned shawl. He stared at Retief, looking him over like a prospective purchaser.

"Well, what about it, Sopp?" the Flink demanded. "You're the best in the business. You think you can do it?"

"Well . . . I can give it a try."

"Great!" the Flink chirped. "If this works, it'll be the slickest caper pulled in his town since you rigged Geeper out as a Blint and he fertilized half the rolling stock in the Municipal Car-Barns!"

"Well," the Yerkle said two hours later. "It's not perfect, but in a bad light you may pass."

"Sopp, it's your masterpiece." The Flink, whose name was Ibbl, rolled in a circle around Retief. "If I didn't know different, I'd swear he was some kind of a cross-

46

breed Jorp in town for the bright lights! That set of trimmed-down Twilch rotors is perfect!"

"Just so you don't try to fly," Sopp said to Retief. "It's a wonder to me how some of these life-forms get around, with nothing but chemical energy to draw on. I've tucked a few Terry food bars in the hip pouch to help keep you running."

Creaking slightly, Retief stepped to the nearest window, a roughly hexagonal panel of rippled amber glass, backed by a closed shutter of dark wood. His reflection, distorted by the uneven surface, was startling: curving plates of deep maroon metallo-chitin had been snipped, warped, then neatly welded to form a suit of smoothly articulated armor which covered him from neck to toe. Over his hands, Sopp had fitted a pair of massive red snipping claws salvaged from a Grunk, operable from within by a system of conveniently arranged levers, while a dummy abdominal section from a defunct Clute, sprayed to match the over-all color scheme, disguised the short Terran torso. A handsome set of vestigial pink wing cases edged in a contrasting shade of purplish black lent a pleasant accent to the shoulder region that went far to camouflage their width. The headpiece, taken from a prime specimen of the Voion tribe, sprayed a metallic red-orange and fitted with a crest of pink-dyed Jarweel plumes, fitted lightly over Retief's face, a hinged section closing down to clamp in place behind.

"Of course, those big, long, thick legs are a bit odd," Sopp said. "But with the rotating members adapted for rotor use, naturally the anterior arms have to fill in as landing gear. There's a few tribes that have gone in for stilting around, and developed them into something quite useful."

"Sure," Ibbl agreed. "Look at the Terries: no wheels, but they manage OK. I tell you, he looks like a natural! Outside of a few unreconstructed Voion trying to flog him a set of solid gold inlays or some snappy photos of the tribal ovumracks, nobody'll give him a second look."

"Gentlemen," Retief said, "you've produced a miracle. It's even comfortable. All it needs now is a service test."

"Where will you go? Ikk's got the whole town sewed up tight as a carapace in molting season."

"I'll head for the Terry Embassy. It's not far."

Sopp looked doubtful. "Farther than you think, maybe." He turned to a wall display, selected a two-foot broadsword fashioned from the iridescent wing case of a Blang. "Better take this. It may come in handy to, shall we say, cut your way through the undergrowth."

The long twilight of Quopp was staining the sky in vivid colors now; through a chink in the shutter, Retief saw lights glowing against the shadows blanketing the hushed street where the Voion waited, silent. Up high, the carved façades still caught the light, gleaming in soft pastels against the neon-bright sky.

"I think it's time to go," he said. "While I still have light enough to see where I'm going."

"You want to be careful, Terry." Ibbl was scanning the street from the other window. "Those Voion are in a nasty mood. They're waiting for something. You can feel it in the air."

"I'm subject to moods myself," Retief said. "At the moment I think I could spot them high, low, and jack and still win it in a walkaway." He took a final turn up and down the room, testing the action of the suit's joints; he checked the location of the power pistol with his elbow; it was tucked inconspicuously behind the flare of a lateral hip flange, accessible for a fast draw.

"Thanks again, fellows. If our side wins, the brandies are on me."

"Good luck, Terry. If your side wins, remember me when it's time to let the contract to junk out the police force."

"You'll be first on the list." Retief worked the lever that clacked his anterior mandibles in the gesture of Reluctant Departure on Press of Urgent Business and stepped out into the steet.

It was a brisk fifteen minutes walk to the Path of Many Sporting Agents, every yard of the way impeded by Voion who stared, gave ground reluctantly. Retief came in sight of the Embassy complex, saw Voion clustered before the main doors in a solid mass. He forced his way closer, eliciting complaints from jostled sightseers. Behind the wide glass panels, the darting shapes of Dinks were working busily; a steady stream of Voion were coming and going, with much shrilling of commands and waggling of signals. There were no Terrans in evidence.

Retief pushed into a narrow shop entry across the street from the scene of the activity, scanned the upper Embassy windows. There were lights on there, and once or twice a shape moved behind the colored glass panes.

There was a distant, thudding clatter. Retief looked up, saw the vast shape of an immense flying Rhoon soar on its wide rotors across the strip of sky between buildings, followed a moment later by a second. Then a tiny heli appeared, bilious yellow-green in color, flitting low above the Chancery Tower. As Retief watched, a head appeared over the cockpit rim—the merest glimpse of stalked eyes, a pale throat bladder—

"That one's no Voion, nor no Terry, either," a reedy voice said at Retief's elbow. He looked around to see an aged Kloob, distingushed by a metallic vermillion abdomen and small, almost atrophied wheels.

"Whoever he was, he seems to be on good terms with the Rhoon," Retief said.

"Never saw that before," the Kloob said. "There's unnatural things going on in the world these days: Rhoon flying over town. Like they was patrolling, like."

"I don't see any of the Terry diplomats around," Retief said. "What's been going on here?"

"Ha! What hasn't been going on? First the smoke and the big bang; then the Voion cops swarming all over . . ." The Kloob clacked his ventral plates with a rippling noise indicating total lack of approval. "Things are coming to a pretty pass when a bunch of Voion trash can take over the Terry Embassy and make it stick."

"So it's like that, eh?" Retief said. "What happened to the Terries?"

"Dunno. I'm taking a short siesta and I wake up and all I can see is cops. Too bad, too. The Terries were good customers. I hate to see 'em go."

"Maybe they'll be back," Retief said. "They've still got a few tricks left."

"Maybe—but I doubt it," the Kloob said glumly. "Ikk's got 'em buffaloed. The rest of us Quoppina better head for the tall grass."

"Not a bad idea. I wonder where I could pick up a map."

"You mean one of those diagrams showing where places are? I've heard of 'em—but I could never quite figure out what they were for. I mean, after all, a fellow knows where he is, right? And he knows where he wants to go . . ."

"That's one of the areas in which we Stilters are a little backward," Retief said. "We seldom know where we are, to say nothing of where we're going. The place I'm looking for is somewhere to the northeast—that way." He pointed.

"More that way." The Kloob indicated a direction three degrees to the right of Retief's approximation. "Straight ahead. You can't miss it. That where your tribe hangs out? Never saw one like you before."

"There's a group of my tribesfellows in trouble out there," Retief said. "About eighty miles from here."

Hm. That's a good four days on a fast Blint if the trails are in shape."

"How does the port look?"

"Guards on every gate. The Voion don't want any of us traveling, looks like."

"I'm afraid I'll have to argue that point with them."

The Kloob looked dubiously at Retief. "Well, I can guess who'll win the argument—but good luck to you anyway, Stilter."

Retief pushed through the loosely milling crowd for half a block before one of the stick-twirling Planetary Police thrust out an arm to halt him.

"You, there! Where are you going?" He hummed in Voion tribal.

"Back where a fellow can dip a drinking organ in a short Hellrose and nibble a couple of sourballs without some flat-wheel flapping a mandible at him," Retief replied shortly. "One side, you, before I pry that badge off your chest to give to the grubs for a play-pretty."

The Voion retreated. "Tell the other hicks to stay clear of the city," he rasped. "Now get rolling before I run you in."

Retief thrust past him with a contemptuous snap of his left chela. The sun was almost down now, and few lamps had gone on in the shops to light the way. There were no other Quoppina in sight, only the sullen black of the Voion, many of them with the crude shell inlays and filed fangs of tribesmen. The port, Retief estimated, would be off to the right, where the last purplish gleam of sunset still showed above the building tops. He headed that way, one elbow touching the butt of the power gun.

Clustered polyarcs gleamed down from tall poles to reflect on the space-scarred hulls of half a dozen trade vessels as Retief came up to the sagging wire fence surrounding the port. More lights gleamed by the gate where four Voion were posted, twirling clubs.

"Which one of you blackwheels do I bribe to get in?" Retief called out in Tribal.

All four Voion spoke at once; then one waved an arm for silence. "I'm corporal of the guard here, rube," he buzzed. "What have you got in mind?"

"Well, now, what's the going price?" Retief sauntered casually to a position two yards from the open gate.

"You talking Village, or Terry credit?"

"Do I look like I'm hauling thirty or forty pounds of Rock around with me?" Retief inquired. "I just peddled a cargo of country booze down at the barracks. I've got enough Terry credit to hang the four of you with."

"Have you, now?" The quartet shifted positions to encircle Retief, a move which placed two of them farther from the gate then himself.

"You bet." He reached into the pouch slung at his hip, pulled out a tangle of plastic, gained another step toward the corporal, who canted his oculars at the cash.

"Here, catch." Retief tossed the credit. As the NCO reached to snare it, the other three Voion said "hey!" and converged on him. Retief stepped through the gate, slammed it, clicked the hanging padlock shut, leaving the four guards outside.

"Hold on there, you!" the corporal keened. "You can't go in there!"

"I figured you sharpies would hold out on me," Retief said. "Well, I'm in now. You can yell for the sergeant and turn the bundle over to him, or you can forget you saw me and work out a fair split. So long."

"Hey," one of the Voion said. "Look at the way that Stilter walks! Like a Terry, kind of . . ."

"Are you kidding?" the corporal inquired.

"Look, fellows, the way I see it, what's it to us if this yokel wants to sight-see . . . ?"

Retief moved off as the foursome settled down to quarreling over the loot, headed for the nearest of the five ships in sight, a battered thousand tonner with the purple and yellow comet insignia of the Four Planet Line. The few lounging locals in sight ignored him as he went to the rear access ladder, swung up and stepped inside. A startled Voion looked up from a little of papers and clothes spilled from a locker, the door of which had been pried from its hinges. As the looter reached for a club lying on a table, Retief caught his outstretched arm, spun him around, planted a foot against his back, and launched him toward the open entry. The Voion emitted a thin screech as he shot through, yelped as he hit the pavement below with a splintering crash.

Retief swarmed up the ladder to the cargo deck, rode the one-man lift to the control compartment, cycled the other lock shut, then quickly checked gauges.

"Swell," he said softly. "Just enough fuel to stage a blazing reentry." He whirled to the lifeboat bay, cycled the hatch. Two tiny one-man shells rested in their slings. Retief wiped dust from the external inspection panel of the nearest, saw the dull red glow of panic lights indicating low accumulator charge, a leaky atmosphere seal, and over-aged fuel. He checked the second boat; its accumulators read full charge, though it, too, was leaking air and indicating a decayed fuel supply. Retief went back to the panel, flipped a key, glanced at the ground-view screens. Voion were closing in on the vessel from three sides; he recognized the evicted impulse shopper in the van, limping on an out-of-round wheel.

He went back to the Number Two lifeboat, popped the canopy, climbed inside, fitted himself into the cramped seat, taking care to settle his rotors and wing cases comfortably, then closed the hatch. He activated the warm-up switch; panel lights blinked on. The boat was flyable —maybe. Retief kicked in the eject lever and slammed back in the padded seat as the rocket blast hurled the tiny boat skyward.

Level at five thousand feet, Retief set a northeast course. As he looked back at the pattern of city lights below, a brilliant red light glowed, climbed upward from a point near the center of the town, burst in a shower of whirling pin-wheels of green, yellow, magenta. A second rocket went up, then three together, more, shedding a carnival glow over the clustered towers of the city. Retief punched a button on the tiny panel, twirled a dial.

". . . laration of the establishment of a new era of Quopp-wide peace and plenty," a voice boomed from the radio, "under the benign and selfless leadership of His Omnivoracity, our glorious leader, Prime Minister Ikk! All loyal Quoppina are instructed to remain in their village or other place of residence until tax assessors, draft board officials, and members of the emergency requisition team have completed initial surveys. All citizens will be required to purchase a copy of *New Laws and Punishments,* for sale at all newsstands for a low, low nine ninety-eight, plus tax. Failure to possess a copy will be punishable by Salvage. And now, a word from our effulgent chief, the great liberator of Quopp, Prime Minister Ikk!"

There was a prolonged burst of shrill prerecorded applause that made Retief's eardrums itch, then the familiar tones of the Voion leader:

"Fellow Voion, and you other, shall I say, honorary Voion," he started. "Now that the planet is free, certain changes will be made; no longer will the unenlightened struggle on, following erroneous tribal customs! We Voion have figured out all the answers, and—"

Retief flicked off the radio, settled down for the eighty mile run ahead.

The lifeboat rocked abruptly, as though it had glanced off a giant, spongy pillow. Retief banked to the right, scanned the sky above. A wide, dark shape swooped quickly past; there was a sudden buffeting as the small craft pitched in the backwash of the thirty-foot rotors of a giant Rhoon. It swung in a wide circle, climbing, then pivoted sharply, stooped again, hurtling straight at him like a vast pouncing eagle. Retief slammed the controls full over, felt the lifeboat flip on its back, drop like a stone toward the jungle below. He rolled out, shot away at full thrust, at right angles to his previous course. Off to the right the Rhoon tilted up in a sharp turn, faint starlight gleaming from its spinning rotors, swelling enormously as it closed. Again Retief dove under it, pulled out to find it close on his port side, angling in across his bows. He gave the boat full throttle, shot under the Rhoon's yellow-green head, then pulled the nose up, climbing. . . .

The skiff was sluggish under him, staggering; he reduced the angle of climb, saw the Rhoon dropping in from his port quarter. Again he dived, leveled out this time a scant thousand feet above the dark jungle below. A glance to the right showed the Rhoon banking in for another pass; its mighty rotors drove it effortlessly at twice the speed the skiff could manage on its outdated fuel. Retief saw its four ten-foot-long armored fighting members, its gaping jaws armed with saw-edged fangs that could devour any lesser Quoppina in two snaps. At the last moment, he rolled to the right, went over on his back, snapped out of the maneuver to whip off to the left, coming around sharply on the Rhoon's flank. With a jerk at the release handle, he jettisoned the canopy; it leaped clear with a dull boom, and a tornado of air whipped at Retief's face. He jerked the power gun clear of its holster, took aim, and as the Rhoon banked belatedly to the right, fired for the left rotor. Yellow light glared from the whipping blades as Retief held the beam full on the spinning hub; a spot glowed a dull red; then a puff of vapor whiffed up—and suddenly the air was filled with whining fragments, whistling past Retief's exposed head and ricocheting off the skiff's hull. Retief held the beam on target another five seconds, saw the Rhoon tilt almost vertically, vibrating wildly as the damaged rotor shook itself to pieces; something small and dark seemed to break from the Rhoon then, clung for a moment, dropped free. Then the great predator was on its back, a glimpse of gray belly plates and folded legs, then gone as the boat shot past. At that moment, a violent shock slammed Retief hard against the restraining harness. He grabbed the controls, fought to pull the boat up. A flat expanse of black wilderness swung up past the nose, rolled leisurely over the top, then slid down the left side. . . .

The controls bit into the air then; fighting vertigo, Retief hauled the boat out of the spin. The motor barked once, twice, snarled unevenly for a moment, then died.

The ship bucked, wanting to fall off on its port stub-wing. A glance showed torn metal, a dark stain of leaking coolant. The skiff was no more than a hundred feet above tree level now; ahead a tall spike-palm loomed. Retief banked to the right, felt the boat drop under him. He caught a momentary glimpse of the immense wreckage of the Rhoon strewn across half an acre of bushy treetops; then he was crashing through yielding foliage, the boat slamming left, then right, then upended, tumbling, dropping to a final splintering crash of metalwood, a terrific impact that filled the tiny cockpit with whirling fireworks even brighter than the ones over the city, before they faded into a darkness filled with distant gongs. . . .

4

Something sharp poked Retief in the side, a vigorous jab that bruised even through the leather strip that joined the dorsal and ventral plates of his costume. He made an effort, sat up, reached to investigate the extent of the skull fracture, felt the metallic clang as his claw touched the painted Voion headpiece. The tough armor, it seemed, had its uses. He pushed the helmet into alignment, looked around at a torch-lit clearing among the boles of great trees, and a ring of three-foot blue-green Quoppina, members, he saw, of the Ween tribe, all eyeing him with faintly luminous oculars, their saber-like fighting claws ready, their scarlet biting apparatus cleared for action.

"Hoo. Meat-fall-from-sky moving around," a tiny, penetrating voice keened in heavily accented Tribal. "Us better slice it up quick, before it get clean away."

Retief got to his feet, felt for the gun with his elbow. It was gone—lost in the crash. One midget meat-eater, bolder than the rest, edged closer, gave a tentative snap of his immense white-edge claw. Retief worked levers, clacked back at him.

"Stand back, little fellow," he said. "Don't you recognize a supernatural apparition when you see one?" He moved to put his back to a tree.

"What you mean, big boy?" one of the natives demanded. "What that big word mean?"

"It means it's bad medicine to cook a stranger," Retief translated.

"Hmm, that mean we is got to eat you raw. How is you, tough?"

Retief drew the short sword. "Tough enough to give you a bellyache, I'd estimate."

"Hey, what kind of Quopp is you, anyway?" someone inquired. "I ain't never see one like you before."

"I'm a diplomat," Retief explained. "We mostly lie up during the day and come out at night to drink."

"A Dipple-mac. Hmmm. Ain't never heard of that tribe before, is you, Jik-jik?"

"Can't say as I is. Must come from over the mountain."

"How you get here, Meat-from-sky?" somebody called. "You ain't got the wingspan for no flying."

"In that." Retief nodded toward the smashed shell of the skiff.

"What that?" one native inquired. Another prodded the machine with a small wheel, adapted for rough jungle trails. "Whatever it is, it dead." He looked at Retief. "You friend no help to you now, big boy. You is all alone."

"You a long way out of your territory, Stilter," another said. "Ain't never see one like you before. What you doing here in Ween country?"

"I'm just passing through," Retief said. "I'm looking for a party of Terrans that wandered off-course. I don't suppose you've seen them?"

"I heard of them whatchacallums—Terrans. They twelve feet high and made out of jelly, I hears; and they takes their wheels off at night and leaves 'em outside."

"That's the group. Any sign of them in these parts?"

"Nope," the Ween crossed their rear oculars, indicating negation.

"In that case, if you'll stand aside, I'll breeze on my way and let you get back to whatever you were doing when I dropped in."

"What we was doing, we was starving, Meat-from-sky. Your timing good."

"Jik-jik, you all the time talking to something to eat,"

someone said from the ranks. "What you all say to a nice barbecue sauce on this meal, with greens on the side?"

There was a sudden flurry of sound from the near distance, punctuated by shrill cries.

"Get your feather-picking members off me, you ignorant clodhoppers!" a thin Voion voice screeched. "I'm a member of the Planetary Armed Forces! There's a big reward—" The speech cut off in mid-sentence; threshing sounds followed. Moments later, three Ween pushed into the clearing, hauling the limp figure of a bright-polished member of the Planetary Police. He groaned as they dropped him; one of his wheels, badly warped, whirled lopsidedly.

"Hoo, this evening shaping up," someone said. The Voion was lying on his back, waving all four arms feebly.

"You can't do this to me," the captive tweeted. "In the name of the Wo—" The Ween standing closest to the fallen policeman brought his immense claw around and with a sound like a pistol shot nipped off the newcomer's head with a single snap.

"Well, that the first of them big noises I see trimmed up like he ought to be," Jik-jik said. "You got him just in time, Fut-fut, before he call on the Name of the Worm—" He broke off, looked at Retief.

"In the Name of the Worm," Retief said, "what about a little hospitality?"

"You and your big vocalizing apparatus," someone said disgustedly. "Well, back to camp. At least us can fry up some policeman to tide us over." A quartet of Ween lifted the limp body; someone picked up the head.

"Lucky for you you call on the Name of the Worm," Jik-jik said conversationally. "Old Hub-hub ready to dine right now, what I mean."

"Mentioning the Worm takes me off the menu, eh?"

"Well, it give you time to get you thoughts in order, anyway."

"I have a feeling that remark is pregnant with meanings, none of them pleasant."

"Hoo, it simple enough, big boy. It mean us keep you pen up for five days, and then skin you out for a old-fashioned tribal blowout."

An aggressive-looking Ween pushed forward. "How

about if us trim off a few edges now—just to sample the flavor?"

"Get back there, Hub-hub," Jik-jik admonished. "No snacking between meals."

"Come on, Meat-from-sky," the aggressive pygmy called. "Get you wheels in gear." He reached out with his claw to prod Retief—and jumped back with a screech as the heavy sword whipped down, lopped off an inch of the member's pointed tip.

"Look what he do to my chopper!" he shrilled.

"You ask for it, Hub-hub," Fut-fut said.

"I like a lot of space around me," Retief said, swinging the sword loosely in his hand. "Don't crowd me."

The Ween edged back, fifty or more small, dark-glittering creatures like oversized army ants in a wide ring around Retief, his armor a splash of vivid color in the gloom. Hub-hub jittered, holding his damaged claw high, torchlight glinting on his metallic sides. "I is hereby taking this piece of meat off the chow list!" he screeched. "I is promoting him to the status of folks!"

"Hey, Hub-hub, is you gone out of you head? What the idea of doing a trick like that . . . ?" A chorus of protest broke out.

Jik-jik confronted the outraged tribesman.

"He chop off a piece of you, and now you chumming up to him. What the idea?"

"The idea is now I ain't got to wait no five days to get a piece back!" Hub-hub keened. "Get back, all of you . . ." He waved the two-foot long, steel-trap claw in a commanding gesture. "I is now going to snip this Stilter down to size!"

The Ween drew back, disappointed but obedient to tribal custom. Hub-hub danced before Retief, who waited, his back to the tree, the sword held before him, torchlight glinting along its steel-hard razor-sharp edge. Hub-hub darted in, legs twinkling, snick-snacked a double feint high and low with the big fighting arm, lashed out viciously with a pair of small pinchers, then struck with the big claw, eliciting a loud clang! from Retief's chest armor—and staggered as the flat of Retief's blade knocked him spinning.

"Hoo!" Jik-jik shrilled. "Old Hub-hub chew off more than he can bite this time!"

"Let's call this off, Shorty," Retief suggested. "I'd hate to have to skewer you before we've really gotten acquainted—"

The Ween danced in, pivoting on spider legs, feinted, struck with his fighting claw—

Retief's sword flashed in a lightning arc, sang as it bit through steel-hard metallo-chitin. The oversized claw dropped to the ground.

"He . . . he done chop off my chopper . . . !" Hub-hub said faintly. "Now he going stick me for sure . . ." He crouched, waiting, a drop of syrupy dark fluid forming on the stump.

"Serve you right, Hub-hub," someone called.

"Suppose I let you go?" Retief stepped forward and prodded the Ween's slender neck with the sword point. "Promise to be good and speak only when spoken to?"

"Way I feels now, I done talking for good," Hub-hub declared.

"Very well." Retief lowered the blade. "Go with my blessing."

"Well, that a neat trick, big boy," Jik-jik commented. "Take him six months to grow a new arm, and meantime he learn to keep his mandibles buttoned."

Retief looked around. "Anybody else?' he inquired. There were no takers.

"In that case, I'll be on my way. You're sure you haven't noticed a ship crashing in the vicinity in the past few hours?"

"Well, now, that different," Jik-jik stated. "They was a big smash over yonder way a while back. We was looking for it when we found you, Stilter."

"The name's Retief. Now that we're all friends and tribesfellows, how about a few of you showing me the spot where it came down?"

"Sure, Tief-tief. It not far from where you was."

Retief walked over to examine the body of the decapitated Voion. He had obviously been a member of Ikk's police—or army—complete with brand-new chromalloy inlays and an enameled cranium insignia with a stylized picture of what looked like a dragonfly.

"I wonder what this fellow was doing out here, so far from town," Retief said.

"I don't know," Jik-jik said; "but I got a feeling when us finds out us ain't going like it."

The bright disk of Joop was high above the treetops, shedding a cold white light on the village street. Retief followed as Jik-jik and two other tribesmen led the way along a trail worn smooth by the wheels of generations of forest dwellers. It was a fifteen minute trek to the spot where Pin-pin halted and waved an arm. "Yonder's where I found that policeman," he said. "Back in the brush. I heard him cussing up a cyclone back there."

Retief pushed through, came to a spot where fallen limbs and scattered leaves marked the position of the injured Voion. Above, the silvery ends of broken branches marked a trajectory through the treetops.

"What I wondering, how he get up there?" Pin-pin inquired. "Funny stuff going on around here. Us heard the big crash—that why us out here—"

"The big crash—which way was that?" Retief asked.

"Yonder," Pin-pin pointed. Again he led the way, guided by the unerring Quoppina instinct for direction. Fifty feet along the trail, Retief stooped, picked up a twisted fragment of heavy, iron-gray metallo-chitin, one edge melted and charred. He went on, seeing more bits and pieces—a bright-edged shred here, swinging from a bush, a card-table-sized plate there, wedged high in a tree. Then suddenly the dull-gleaming mass of a major fragment of the wrecked Rhoon loomed through the underbrush, piled against the ribbed base of a forest giant.

"Hoo, that big fellow hit hard, Tief-tief," Pin-pin said. "Wonder what bring him down?"

"Something he tried to eat disagreed with him." Retief made his way around the giant corpse, noting the blaster burns on the stripped hub of the rotors, the tangle of internal organic wiring exposed by the force of the crash, the twisted and shattered landing members. The rear half of the body was missing, torn away in the passage through the trees.

"Wonder what a Rhoon meet big enough to down him?" Pin-pin wondered. "He the toughest critter in this jungle; everybody spin gravel when a Rhoon flit overhead." The Ween dipped a finger in a smear of spilled lubricant, waved it near an olfactory organ.

"Fool!" he snorted. "That gone plumb rancid already! I guess we don't make no meal off this fellow!"

Retief clambered up the side of the downed behemoth, looked down into an open cavity gouged in the upper side of the thorax, just anterior to the massive supporting structures for the rotating members. Wires were visible; not the irregular-diametered organic conduits of the Quoppina internal organization, but bright-colored cables bearing lettering . . .

"Hey, Tief-tief!" Pin-pin called suddenly. "Us better get scarce! This boy's relations is out looking for him!"

Retief looked up; a great dark shape was visible, hovering a few hundred feet above treetop level. By the bright light of Joop, a second and a third Rhoon appeared, cruising slowly back and forth over the position of their fallen comrade.

"They going to spot him any minute now," Pin-pin said. "I says let's get!"

"They can't land here," Retief said. "They've already spotted him; they're patrolling the location. . . ." He looked around, listening. There was the whine of the breeze among metallac leaves, the high throb of idling Rhoon rotors, a distant rustle of underbrush. . . .

"Somebody's coming," Retief said. "Let's fade back and watch."

"Look Tief-tief, I just remembered, I got a roof needs patching—"

"We'll lie low and pull back if it's more than we can handle, Pin-pin. I don't want to miss anything."

"Well . . ." The three Ween went into a hurried consultation, then clacked palps in reluctant agreement. "OK —but if it's a bunch of them no-good Voion coming to see what can they steal, us leaving," Pin-pin announced. "They getting too quick with them clubs lately."

It was five minutes before the first of the approaching group came into view among the great scarlet- and purple-boled trees, laden with full field packs and spare tires.

"What I tell you?" Pin-pin whispered shrilly. "More of them policemen! They all over the place!"

Retief and the Ween watched as more and more Voion came up, crowding into the clearing leveled by the passage of the Rhoon, all chattering in a subdued buzz, fingering their blackwood clubs and staring about them into the forest.

"Plenty of them," a Ween hissed. "Must is six sixes of sixes if they's a one. . . ."

"More than that. Look at 'em come!"

An imposing-looking Voion with a jewel in his left palp appeared; the others fell back, let him through. He rolled up beside the dead Rhoon, looked it over.

"Any sign of Lieutenant Xit?" he demanded in trade dialect.

"What he say?" Pin-pin whispered.

"He's looking for the one you fellows found," Retief translated.

"Oh-oh; they ain't going to like it if they finds him."

The conversation among the Voion continued:

". . . trace of him, Colonel. But there a native village not far away; maybe they can help us."

The colonel clacked his palps. "They'll help us," he grated. "Which way?"

The Voion pointed. "Half a mile—there."

"All right, let's march." The column formed up, started off in a new direction.

"For a minute I figure they mean Weensville," Pin-pin said. "But they headed for the Zilk town."

"Can we skirt them and get there first?" Retief asked.

"I reckon—but I ain't hungry just now—and besides, with them policemens on the way—"

"I'm not talking about grocery shopping," Retief said. "Those Voion are in a mean mood. I want to warn the villagers."

"But they's Zilk. What we care what happen to them babies?"

"The Terries I'm looking for might be there; I'd prefer to reach them before the Voion do. Beside which, you villagers should stick together."

"Tief-tief, you is got funny ideas, but if that's what you wants . . ."

Retief and his guides pushed through a final screen of underbrush, emerged at the edge of a cleared and planted field where the broad yellow leaves of a ripening crop of alloy plants caught the Jooplight.

"Them Zilk a funny bunch," Pin-pin said. "Eats nothing

but greens. Spends all they time grubbing in the ground."

"In that case, I don't suppose they have to wait until a policeman drops in to plan a meal," Retief pointed out. He started across the open field.

"Hoo, Tief-tief!" Pin-pin hurried after him. "When I say they don't eat folks, that don't mean they don't snap a mean chopper! Us is tangled with them before, plenty of times! You can't just wheel in on 'em!"

"Sorry, Pin-pin. No time for formalities now. Those cops aren't far behind us."

A tall, lean Quoppina appeared at the far side of the field—a bright yellow-orange specimen with long upper arms tipped with specialized earth-workiing members, shorter, blade-bearing limbs below.

"Oh-oh; they sees us. Too late to change our minds now." Jik-jik held his fighting claw straight up in a gesture indicating peaceful intentions.

"What d'ye want here, ye murderous devils?" a high, mellow voice called.

"I'm looking for a party of Terrans whose boat crash-landed near here a few hours back," Retief called. "Have you seen them?"

"Terrans, is it?" the Zilk hooted. "I've not seen 'em— and if I had, I'd not be likely to turn 'em over to the likes o' you."

Other Zilk were popping from the low, domed huts now, fanning out, moving forward on both flanks in an encircling pincer movement. At close range, Retief could see the businesslike foot-long scythes tipping the lower arms.

"Listen here, you Zilk," Jik-jik called in a voice which may have quavered a trifle. "In the Name of the Worm— us ain't just here to ask foolish questions; us is got news for you folks."

"And we've got news for you—not that ye'll ever have the chance to spread it about—"

"Us come to tip you folks off," the Ween persisted. "They a mob of mean-looking Voion on the way! Less you wants to tangle with 'em, you better head for the brush!"

"Don't try to put us off with wild tales, Ween!"

"It's the truth, if I ever told it"

"Why would ye tell us—if t'were true?"

"It beat me; it were Tief-tief here had the idea."

"What kind o' Quoppina is he?" the Zilk called. "I've seen no Stilter wi' half the length o' member that one shows."

"He a out-of-town boy; just passing through."

"T'is a trick, Wikker," a Zilk beside the spokesman hooted. "I'd not trust the little butchers as far as I could kick 'em—nor the big Stilter, neither."

"The Voion are looking for a friend of theirs," Retief said. "They have an idea you'll help them look."

"We'll help 'em off our land," a Zilk stated. "I seen a mort o' the scoundrels about the acreage lately, running in packs and trampling the crops—"

"They're armed and they mean business," Retief said. "Better get ready."

The Zilk were closing in now; the three Ween crowded up against Retief, their fighting claws clicking like castanets. Retief drew his sword.

"You're making a mistake," he told the advancing Zilk leader. "They'll be here any minute."

"A sly trick, ye heathens—but we Zilk are too shrewd for ye—"

"Hey!" A Zilk called. The others turned. The lead elements of the Voion column were just emerging from the forest. At once, the Zilk formation broke, fell back in confusion toward the town.

"Get the females and grubs clear," the Zilk chief honked, and dashed away with the rest. The Voion colonel, seeing the tribesmen in confusion, barked an order; his troops rolled forward through the field, clubs ready.

"Let them have the town." Retief seized the arm of the chief as he shot by. "Disperse in the jungle and you can reform for a counterattack!"

The Zilk jerked free. "Well—maybe. Who'd ha' thought a crowd of Ween were telling the truth?" He rushed away.

The Voion were well into the village now; startled Zilk, caught short, dashed from huts and wheeled for cover burdened with hastily salvaged possessions, only to drop them and veer off, with hoots of alarm, as fast-wheeling Voion intercepted them.

"Us better back off," Jik-jik proposed from the shelter of a hut on the sidelines.

"Scout around and try to round up the survivors," Retief said. "Pin-pin, you make it back to Weensville and bring up reinforcements. The Voion need a little lesson in intertribal cooperation before their success goes to their heads."

Half an hour later, from a screen of narrow pink leaves that tinkled in the light breeze, Retief, several dozen Zilk, and seventy-odd Ween watched by the waning light of the fast-sinking Joop as a swarm Retief estimated at three hundred Voion, a few showing signs of a brisk engagement, prodded their captives into a ragged lineup.

"I don't know what's got into them babies," Jik-jik said. "Used to be they garbage-pickers, slipping around after Second Joop, looking for what they could pick up; now here they is, all shined up and acting like they rule the roost."

"They've gotten a disease called ambition," Retief said. "The form they have causes a severe itch in the acquisitive instinct."

"Not much meat on a Zilk," someone mused. "What you reckon they want over here? Can't be they just looking for they boy; them Voion never frets over no trifles like that."

"Hoo!" Fut-fut said, coming to Retief's side. "Look what they up to now!"

The Voion, having arranged the captive Zilk in two columns of a dozen or so individuals of both sexes, were busy with strips of flexible metallo-plastic, welding shackles to the arms of the first in line, while others of their number poised with raised clubs to punish any resistance. The lead Zilk, seeing the chain about to be linked to him, lashed out suddenly with his scythe, severing a Voion arm at the first joint, then plunged through the circle around him, dashed for the jungle. A Voion wheeled into his path, brought his club around in a whistling arc—and bounced aside as the Zilk snapped out an overlong digging arm, just as two more Voion closed from the off side, brought their clubs down in unison. The Zilk skidded aside, arms whirling, crashed in a heap and lay still.

"Nice try, Wikker," the Zilk chief muttered. "Don't reckon I'd endure chains on me, either."

"That's what happens when you play it their way,"

Retief said. "I suggest we work out some new rules. We'll decoy them into the jungle, break up their formation, and take them one at a time."

"What you mean, Tief-tief? Us going to tackle them ugly babies?"

"Sure, why not?"

"Well, I guess you is right. Us ain't got nothing else scheduled for the evening."

"Good," Retief said. "Now, here's what I've got in mind . . ."

Three Voion working busily to pry the lid from the Zilk town grain bin paused in their labors. Again the thin cry sounded from the forest near at hand.

"Sounds like a lost grub," one said. "A little tender roast meat wouldn't go bad now; pounding in the skull-plates of farmers is hard work."

"Let's take a look. The colonel's busy overseeing the looting; he won't notice us."

"Let's go." The three dropped their pry-bars, wheeled briskly across to the deep shadow of the thicket whence the sound emanated. The first in line thrust branches aside, rolled slowly forward, peering through the shadows. There was a dull *snack!* and he seemed to duck down suddenly. The Voion behind him hurried forward. "Find it?" he inquired, then skidded to a halt. "Juz!" he whistled. "Where's your head . . . ?" Something small and blue-green sprang up before him, a huge claw opening—

At the sound—a sharp *whock!*—the third Voion halted. "Huj?" he called. "Juz? What's go—" A scythe swung in a whistling arc, and his head bounced off to join those of his comrades. Jik-jik and Tupper, the Zilk leader, emerged from the brush.

"Work like a charm," the Ween said. "Let's do it again."

Behind him, Retief turned from surveying the work in progress in the town.

"I think the colonel's beginning to suspect something; he's falling his men in for a roll call. How many have we given haircuts to so far?"

"Half a six of sixes, maybe."

"We'll have to stage a diversion before he figures out what's going on. Tell Fut-fut and his group to wait five

67

minutes, then kick up a disturbance on the far side of the trail we came in on."

Jik-jik keened orders to a half-grown Ween who darted away to spread the word.

"Now we'll string out along the trail. They'll probably come out in single file. Keep out of sight until their lead unit's well past our last man; at my signal, we'll hit them all together and pull back fast."

"It sounds slick. Let's roll."

Three minutes later, as a Voion sergeant continued to bark out names, the small messenger darted up to the position where Retief and Jik-jik waited beside the trail. "Old Fut-fut, he ready, he say," the lad chirped breathlessly. "Hey, Jik-jik, can I get me one?"

"You ain't got the chopper for it, Ip-ip; but you can scout around the other side of the town, and soon as you hear them policemen's heads popping, you set up a ruckus. That'll keep 'em guessing—them that still has guessing equipment. Now scat; it's time for the fun to begin."

A shrill yell sounded from Fut-fut's position, then an angry yammer of Ween voices, accompanied by sounds of scuffling. From his concealment behind a yard-wide tree with a trunk like pale blue glass, Retief saw a stirring in the Voion ranks as they looked toward the outcry. The colonel barked an order. A squad of Voion fell out, rolled quickly to the trail mouth. There was a moment of confusion as the troops milled, not liking the looks of the dark tunnel; then, at a shrill command from a sergeant, they formed a single file and started in. The first rolled past Retief's position, his club swinging loosely in his hand; he was followed closely by another, and another. Retief counted twenty before they stopped coming. He stepped from behind the tree, glanced toward the village; the roll call went on. He drew his sword, put two fingers in his mouth, and gave a shrill blast. At once, there was a crash of underbrush, a staccato volley of snicks and snaps, followed in an instant by a lone Voion yell, quickly cut off. The last Voion in the column, ducking back from the attacking Ween, spun, found himself confronting Retief. He brought his club up, gave a shrill yelp as Retief, with a roundhouse stroke, cut through the weapon near the grip.

"Go back and tell the colonel he has two hours to get

to town," Retief said. "Any Voion found loose in the jungle after that will be roasted over a slow fire." He implemented the command with a blow of the flat of the blade that sent the Voion wobbling villageward; then he whirled and plunged into the dense growth, made for a vantage point overlooking the village.

There was a high-pitched cry from the far side of the town—Ip-ip at work. The Voion were milling now, unsettled by the sudden noises. The one whose club Retief had clipped off charged into the midst of the platoon, shrilling and waving the stump of the weapon.

". . . forest demon," he was yelling. "Nine feet high, with wheels like a juggernaut, and a head like a Voion, except it was red! Hundreds of them! I'm the only one got away . . . !"

Branches rustled and clanked as Jik-jik came up. "Hoo, Tief-tief, you quite a strategist. Got a passel of the trash that time! What's next?"

The colonel was shrilling orders now, the roll call abandoned; Voion scurried to and fro in confusion.

"Let them go. I see they're not bothering with their prisoners."

The Voion were streaming away down the wide trail in considerable disorder, flinging loot aside as they went. In two minutes the village was deserted, with the exception of the ranks of chained Zilk, staring fearfully about, and the crumpled bodies of their relatives.

"We'll go in quietly so as not to scare them to death," Retief said. "And remember, the idea is to make allies of them; not hors d'oeuvres."

Fifty-one Zilk, three of them badly dented, had survived the attack. Now they sat in a circle among their rescuers, shaking their heads mournfully, still not quite at ease in the presence of seventy fighting Ween.

"Ye warned us, I'll gi' ye that," one said ruefully. "Never thought I'd see the day a bunch of Voion'd jump us Zilk, face to face—even if they did have us six to one."

"The Voion have a new mission in life," Retief said. "Their days of petty larceny are over. Now they're after a whole planet."

"Well, I guess we fix them, hey Tief-tief?" Jik-jik

chuckled. "The way them babies run, they going to need retreads before they gets to town."

"That was just a minor scuffle," Retief said. "They're shaken up at the moment, but they'll be back."

"You sure enough reckon?" Fut-fut executed a twitch of the palps indicating sudden alarm.

"For a Stilter what just hit town at First Joop, you sure is take in a lot of ground in a hurry," Jik-jik said plaintively. "If you knowed them rascals coming back, how come you tell us to mix in in the first place?"

"I thought it would save a lot of talk all around if you Ween saw a demonstration of Voion tactics first hand. Then, too, it seemed worthwhile to help out the Zilk."

"We lost good old Lop-lop," Jik-jik pointed out. "His head plumb bashed in. He was a good eater."

"They lost thirty-five club swingers," Retief said. "We've gained fifty-one new recruits."

"What that?" Jik-jik clacked his secondary claws with a br-r-rapp! "You ain't talking about these here greens-eaters . . . ?"

"Why, ye murderin spawn o' the mud devil, d'ye think we Zilk'd have any part of ye'r heathen ways?" one of the rescuees hooted, waving his scythe. "Ye can all——"

"Hold it, fellow," Retief said. "If it comes to a fight with the city boys, you tribes will stick together or lose. Which will it be?"

"Where you get a idea like that, Tief-tief? They always been a few Voion sneaking around, getting they antennae in——"

"'Just before I arrived here, Ikk declared himself proprietor of the planet; if the rest of you are good, he promises to make you honorary Voion."

There was a chorus of indignant buzzes and hoots from Ween and Zilk alike.

"Well, I'm glad to see an area of agreement at last," Retief said. "Now, if you Zilk are recovered, we'd better be pulling out——"

"What about our crop?" Tupper protested. "It's all ready to harvest——"

"This here grass?" Jik-jik contemptuously plucked a wide golden leaf from the row beside him, waved it under his olfactory organ. "Never could figure out what a Quoppina thinking of, all the time nibbling leaves . . ." He paused, sniffed at the leaf again. Then he bit off a piece with a sound like sardine can being torn in two, chewed thoughtfully.

"Hey," he said. "Maybe us been missing something. This plumb good!"

Fut-fut snorted his amusement, plucked a leaf and sniffed, then bit.

"Hoo!" he announced. "Taste like prime Flink, dog if it don't!"

In a moment, every Ween in sight was busily sampling the Zilk greens.

"Don't s'pose it matters," a Zilk grumbled. "We'll never get the crop in anyway, wi' these Voion robbers on the loose."

"Don't worry about that," a Ween called. "Us'll have these here greens in in ten minutes flat!"

Jik-jik nodded, still masticating. "Maybe us Ween and you Zilk could work together after all," he said. "Us'll do the fighting and you fellows grow the greens."

Retief, Jik-jik, and Tupper watched by the trail as the last of the grubs were carted away by nervous mothers to shelter in the deep jungle along with the village pots and pans, and the newly acquired store of alloy plants. Suddenly Tupper pointed.

"Look up there," he boomed. "A flight of Rhoon—big ones! Coming this way!"

"Scatter!" Retief called. "Into the woods and regroup on the trail to the north!"

Ween and Zilk darted off in every direction. Retief waited until the lead Rhoon had dropped to almost treetop level, heading for a landing in the village clearing; then he faded back into the shadows of the jungle. One by one ten great Rhoon settled in, their rotors flicking back glints of Jooplight as they whirled to a stop. In the gloom, dark figures moved: Voion, filing out from between the parked leviathans, forming up a loose ring among the deserted huts, fanning outward, clubs ready.

"Come on, Tief-tief," Jik-jik said softly. "If them Rhoon wants the place I says let 'em have it—" He broke off. "Look there!" he hissed. "Voion—swarms of 'em— wheeling right under them big babies' snappers!"

"They got here a little sooner than I expected," Retief

said softly. "They must have already set up a field HQ nearby."

"Tief-tief, you know what I'm thinking? I'm thinking them Voion and them Rhoon is working together! But they can't! Ain't no tribe never worked with no other tribe, not since the Worm's first Wiggle!"

"The Ween and the Zilk got together," Retief pointed out. "Why not the Voion and the Rhoon?"

"But that ain't fair, Tief-tief! Ain't nobody can fight a Rhoon! And they always been such peaceable babies. Just set on their mountaintops and leave the flatland to us."

"It seems they've changed their ways. We'll have to fall back. Spread the word to the troops to move off—and keep it quiet."

"Sure is getting dark fast," Jik-jik commented nervously. "Us Ween figure it bad luck to move around in the dark of Joop."

"It'll be worse luck if we stay here. They're forming up to sweep this stretch of jungle clear."

"Well—if you says so, Tief-tief," Jik-jik conceded. "I'll spread the word."

Half an hour later, the party paused on the trail, in total darkness now.

Tupper was peering through the blackness. "I'd give a pretty to know where we are," he said. "Stumping along a trail in the dark—'tis no fit occupation for a sane Quopp."

"We'll have to call a halt until Second Jooprise," Retief said. "We can't see where we're going, but neither can the Voion. They're not using torches either."

"But I can hear 'em; they're not far behind us—the night-crawling heathen!"

"It'll be Second Jooprise in another half hour, maybe," Jik-jik said. "I hopes them Voion is as smart as we is and set still for a while instead of cooking up surprises."

"I don't like it," Tupper stated. "There's something about this spot—I got a feeling hostile eyes are on me!"

"They'll be hostile clubs on you, if you keeps talking so loud," Jik-jik said. "Hush up now and let's all set and rest whiles we can."

Tupper was moving carefully about in the darkness. "Oh-oh," he said softly.

"What that?" Jik-jik demanded.

"It feels like . . ."

"What it feel like?" Jik-jik asked breathlessly.

"Tief—better give us a light," Tupper said tensely.

Retief stepped to his side, took out a lighter, fired a torch supplied by a Ween. The oily brand flared up, cast dancing light on a purplish-gray mound blocking the path.

"Was there something?" a deep voice boomed out.

"Now we is done it," Jik-jik choked out. "Us is right smack dab in the middle of Jackooburg!"

5

At once, a dozen torches flared ahead; Retief looked around at a sprawling collection of wide mud and leaf sheds spotted at random under the shelter of a grove of vast green-barked nicklewood trees. There was a wide yard, beaten to concrete smoothness by heavy wheels; about it were parked a dozen massive, low-slung creatures, five feet at the shoulder and ten feet long, with dusty magenta back plates, foot-thick rear wheels a yard in diameter, and a pair of smaller wheels forward, evolved from the lower pair of arms. The upper arms, flexible and spade-tipped, were coiled under the wide, flat duckbilled heads.

"Well?" the same voice, like heavy syrup, insisted. "I hope you have *some* excuse for bursting in on our nightly contemplation hour!"

"Just leaving, big boy," Jik-jik spun his wheels backward, raising dust that roiled in the torchlight. With a low rumble, a pair of Jackoo wheeled to cut off retreat. Another pair gave low, rumbling honks, took up positions flanking the intruders on the left. More Jackoo appeared from the darkness and still more emerged from shelter among the trees ringing the yard.

"Not in such a darned hurry, skinny-wheels," the Jackoo purred. "Before I roll you out into a pretty orange rug, I'd like to know what you thought you could snitch here."

"I'm looking for a missing party of Terrans," Retief said. "Have you seen them?"

"Terrans? What on Quopp are those?"

"A type of Stilter; they look a little like me, actually, except that they have tender skins."

"Hmm. Sounds tasty. Tell you what; whoever catches them first divvies up with the others, all right?"

"They're not to be eaten," Retief corrected. "I want them whole."

"Oh, greedy, eh?" More Jackoo rolled to complete the encirclement.

"Oh-oh," Jik-jik twittered. "Us surrounded."

"That's fine," Retief said. "Now we won't have any Voion sneaking up on us."

"Tief-tief, us don't want to tangle with those boys," Jik-jik hissed. "They is tough customers. They ain't fast on they wheels, but when they starts, it take a mountain to stop 'em. They flatten whatever they meets!"

"Good. They'll make excellent heavy armor."

"Tief-tief, you is got strange ideas. These Jackoo ain't got a friend in the jungle. They grubbers, and they don't care what kind they gets—Ween, Zilk, Flink—"

"Maybe we can offer them a change of diet."

"If you have any last words, better get them said." The Jackoo were closing in, ponderous as Bolo combat units.

"You boys is got wrong ideas," Jik-jik crowded against Retief. "Us just dropped in to say howdy. I mean, us figured—I mean Tief-tief figured—"

"What he means is," Tupper amplified hastily, "the club-swinging rogues ha' carried out a dastardly attack on Zilk Town, and—"

"And you boys is next," Jik-jik added. "So—"

"Heavens, one at a time!" the Jackoo bellowed. "Gracious, a person can't even hear himself think! Now, let me get this straight: Just which of you is offering what others for sale?"

"The cute one with the long stilts," a Jackoo suggested from the background. "He's the owner, and these other two—"

"Nonsense, Fufu; the sour-looking one owns the squatty one, and the Stilter is some kind of a flack—"

"You're both wrong," a third hollow voice chimed in. "The little jumpy one with the big bitey thing obviously—"

"Gentlemen . . ." Retief held up both gauntleted hands. "I wonder if you've noticed a small conflagration in the near distance?"

"Gracious, yes," the Jackoo named Fufu said. "I thought it was morning and woke up hour early."

"A large party of Voion calling themselves Planetary Police have raided Zilk Town. They'll be here next."

"Well, dandy! Maybe they'll have some succulent grubs for sale. Last time—"

"This isn't like last time," Retief said. "They're not small-time free-lance bushrangers anymore; they've incorporated as a government and gone into the wholesale end. They've started off by levying a modest hundred percent property tax; after collecting that, they draft the survivors into government service, in what capacity we haven't yet determined."

"Ummm, no," the nearest Jackoo thumped heavy palps together in the gesture of Invitation Declined. "We're content as we are, living our peaceful, contemplative lives, bothering no one—"

"What about all them grubs you steals?" Jik-jik put in.

"Well, if you're going to be *picky* . . ."

"What Fufu means is that we don't want to sign up for the program," a Jackoo explained. "Naturally, we think enterprise is ducky, but—"

"It's not exactly an invitation," Retief said. "More of an ultimatum. Your village is on their route of march. They should be here by First Jooprise."

"Well, they'll just have their trouble for nothing," Fufu snorted. "Having one salesman call is one thing, but whole squads of them is simply out of the question!"

"Sure is glad us settle this thing when us did," Pin-pin said heartily. "Now us better disappear in a hurry. Them Voion done snuck up on us; they about six deep all the way around the town."

"I just remembered," Jik-jik said. "I got cousins on the far side of the valley. I believes I'll just go pay them Ween a call—"

76

"Hey, that a good idea, Jik-jik," a nearby Ween chimed in. "Ain't seen old Grandpa since I a nipper. I believes I'll just go along . . ."

"It a shame the way us been neglecting our kin . . ." another offered.

"I has a yen to travel myself . . ." a third realized aloud.

"Hold on," Retief called as a general surge toward the surrounding foliage gathered force. "Running away won't help. The Voion will catch you, whichever way you go."

"It was satisfying, getting the hook into a few o' the murdering no-goods," Tupper keened. "But there's too many o' 'em; our only chance is to slip off, quiet-like . . ."

"Why, you bunch of spoilsports!" Fufu honked. "Do you mean you're going to run away just because a few worthless lightweights might be decapitated?"

"Us worthless lightweights wheeling out of here while the wheeling good," Fut-fut declared. "Rest of you can do what you likes; it a free country!"

"That's right, Tief-tief," Jik-jik sighed. "You Dipplemacs is good fighters, but us knows when us licked."

"Just listen to them chatter," Fufu grunted. "A shameful display of arrant cowardice. Luckily, we Jackoo are simply too brave for words. Unfortunately, we can't see in the dark, so we'll have to bow out of night operation. In fact, I think it might be a good idea to slip quietly away to quieter territory now and recharge our plates. It *has* been rather an unsettling evening—"

"Gentlemen," Retief called, "you're all talking like idiots. They have us hemmed in on all sides. There's only one way to get out of this trap—and that's fight our way out."

"How in the world did we get mixed up in this, Fufu?" a Jackoo boomed. "Why don't we just mash these noisy creatures and get back to sleep?"

"Listen at them," Jik-jik said. "They ready to quit. Only us Ween doing any fighting talk. Too bad we is got to sneak off with the rest of them—"

"Ween, ha!" Tupper shrilled. "Tief-tief's no Ween."

"He a honorary Ween," Jik-jik said sullenly.

"We're wasting time arguing," Retief said. "If we hit them hard, we can punch our way through. They won't be expecting attack."

"I've got an idea," Fufu said. "Since Tief-tief is the one who wants to start trouble, why doesn't he go do it—alone? Then in the confusion, the rest of us can just steal away . . ."

"Hey, that not a bad idea," Jik-jik nodded judiciously. He eased over beside Retief.

"This you big chance to impress me," he whistled. "Not only will you hog all the glory, but if you gets anihilated, nobody miss you. What you say?"

"Very well," Retief said. "I'll lead the attack—if you'll permit me to sit on your back, Fufu—and if the rest of you will follow my lead."

"Well . . . us Ween is fighting sons of guns," Jik-jik said. "But seeing as them Zilk done pooped the party . . ."

"It was you Ween started this talk o' desertion," Tupper honked. "We Zilk will stick as long as any o' ye—if you go first, Tief."

"That's settled, then," Retief said. "Sharpen up your cutting edges, everybody, and we'll see what we can do."

"One thing about being a Stilter," Jik-jik said almost enviously, eyeing Retief, sitting astride Fufu. "You sticks up there like you was welded on. Can't no fellow with wheels manage that trick."

"Get ready," Retief called. Brush was stirring across the yard. A big, tall Voion rolled into view, a jewel glinting in one palp. He crossed his upper arms, propped the lower ones on what would have been hips in a vertebrate.

"You, there!" he shrilled in tribal dialect. "This village is under arrest! Now, all of you Jackoo lie down and roll over on your backs, and if you happen to catch those out-of-town agitators under you, so much the better!"

Fufu's oculars, plus both pairs of antennae, snapped erect.

"*What* did he say?"

"He wants you to lie down and play dead," Retief explained.

"A Jackoo lie down? He *must* be having us on," the great creature honked. "Once a Jackoo is off his wheels, he's—well, I shouldn't noise this about, but since we're allies now—"

"I know; he can't get up again."

"Well?" the Voion colonel shrilled. "You have exactly

one minute to do as you're told, or my troops will fire the underbrush and burn you and your village into slag!"

"These huts of yours; they burn pretty well, don't they, Fufu?" Retief inquired.

"Well, we *do* use magnesium-bearing leaves for our roofs; they're light and easy to manage."

"What we going do now, Tief-tief?" Jik-jik demanded. "Them salesmen means business."

"They've formed up a nice envelopment all the way around our position," Retief said. "And they have all the strategic advantages. That leaves it up to us to score a tactical victory."

"What them words mean?" a Ween demanded.

"They mean the Voion have us outnumbered, outgunned, and outflanked; so we'll have to beat the wheels off them in a fashion they're not expecting."

"How we going do that?"

"Just follow my lead."

"I'm waiting!" the Voion screeched.

"Just be patient another ten seconds," Retief said soothingly.

The glow of approaching Jooprise was bright in the east; abruptly the fast-moving body leaped into view, a vivid edge of greenish light that swelled into a white glare as the great disk swept upward.

Retief drew his sword, pointed it at the Voion.

"Let's go, Fufu," he said. The Jackoo leader gave a mighty honk, and with a surge of power lunged into motion—his tribesmen at his back.

Retief could see leaves tremble on the trees ahead as the ground shook to the charge of the forty multiton Quoppina. For a startled moment, the colonel stood his ground. Then he backed, spun, shot into the underbrush a scant ten yards ahead of Fufu. Retief ducked as his mighty mount thundered in among the trees; leafy branches whipped aside with a screech and clatter of twisted metallo-wood. A polished Voion flashed into sight, gunned aside barely in time, whirled to thrust a bright lance head at Retief, who struck it aside, heard a screech cut off abruptly as the next Jackoo in line pounded across the spot where the invader had stood. More Voion were in sight ahead now, scattering before the avalanche of Jackoo. There was a loud *twang!* and a heavy arrow glanced off Retief's chest armor, whined away over his shoulder. Fufu slammed full tilt into a six-inch tree, bounced it aside as though it were a bundle of straw, veered slightly to miss a two-foot trunk, flushed a Voion who darted ahead, tripped, disappeared under Fufu's blind charge. Two Voion popped up at once, leveling lances, Retief crouched low, struck one spear aside with his sword point, saw Fufu's grubber knock the other flying.

Behind and on both sides a heavy crashing of underbrush attested to the presence of other units of Federation heavy armor charging in line abreast. Above, leaves tinkled and clanged to the passage of moving bodies. Reflected Joop-light winked from the accouterments of half-concealed Voion soldiery.

"Wheee!" Fufu hooted. "This is perfectly thrilling! I never thought I'd be charging into battle with a generalissimo sitting on me."

"Just be sure I'm still in place when you charge out again," Retief instructed.

A portable searchlight winked on ahead, silhouetting scurrying Voion against a bluish haze as they rushed to form up a defensive line against the thunder of approaching attackers.

"Oh, that's lovely," Fufu panted. "I can see them ever so much better now!"

The Voion ahead were dashing hither and thither, each seemingly reluctant to hog the glory of placing himself in the path of the oncoming enemy.

"Swing to the left now," Retief called. A Voion shot across the path ahead, whirled, brought a handgun up as Fufu veered to slam the gunner under his wheels. Two more Voion popped up, leaped aside, gave despairing yelps as Fufu's flankers steamrollered them. Fufu was running parallel to the Voion front now, fifty feet inside the besieging line, half a dozen yards behind a tribesfellow. Voion were racing alongside the turf-pounding line now, loosing off arrows which clacked harmlessly off Jackoo armor. One shot in close, fired at Retief, who ducked, thrust with the sword, saw the Voion wobble wildly, go over, bounce high, and slam into a tree.

The crashing of metallo-chitin under horny wheels was like the thundering of a heavy surf, punctuated by belated screeches of alarm as the Voion rear ranks caught glimpses of the doom rushing down at them. Spears arced up, falling as often among the Voion as among the rebellious tribesmen; blasters fired wildly, and here and there a club swung in a vain blow at a racing Quoppina. Then suddenly Fufu was through the main body, slamming past astonished rear-guardsmen who gaped, dithered, fired too late.

"Swing left!" Retief called. "Maybe we can isolate this bunch!"

Now the Jackoo raced parallel to the outer fringes of a sizable detachment of the foe, cut off from the main body. Behind them, the Ween and Zilk who had made their dash trailing close along the lanes opened up by the heavyweights charged on, disappeared into the surrounding forest in hot pursuit of the demoralized main body. Locked in a solid mass of entangled wheels, the entrapped herd cut off by the rebels battled hopelessly to retreat. Those who eluded the freight-train colunm and fled to the shelter of the woods seemed to disappear abruptly as soon as they reached cover.

The Voion captives were now compressed to the consistency of a single interlocked traffic jam, screeching mournfully and huddling back from the patrolling heavyweights.

"Hold it up, Fufu," Retief called. The Jackoo puffed to a halt, wheezing heavily. His tribesmates, following his lead, closed ranks, buzzing and humming, radiating heat like big purple boilers. The ensnarled Voion squalled, drew even closer together as the mighty creatures stared at them, their sides heaving from the run. The few Planetary Police still mobile darted to and fro, then threw down their weapons and huddled against their embattled fellows. Behind Retief, the concealed combat teams emerged from the brush, snappers snapping, scythes waving.

"Fall out for a ten-minute break, gentlemen," Retief addressed his fighters. "They'll be back in a few minutes; but with about three hundred cops in our custody, we may find the opposition in a mood to talk terms."

"Tief-tief, I is got to hand it to you," Jik-jik stated. "Our plan work out pretty good! Us leave a trail of wide, skinny policemens all the way back to where Jackooburg use to be!"

"Used to be?" Jackoo heads turned.

"Sure; what you think that smoke is?"

"Why—they wouldn't dare . . . !"

"Never mind," Jik-jik said. "It wasn't much of a place anyhow. But Tief-tief—like I says, you is a credit to honorary Weenhood; only thing I don't see is, how come you won't let us get on with breaking them Voion down into bite-size? Way they jumbled up, it take 'em six months to figure out whose wheels belongs to which!"

"This bunch we've rounded up is just a small part of the Voion army," Retief pointed out. "We'll get the maximum use from them as negotiating material—but not if they're disassembled."

"Hey, Tief-tief . . . !" A Ween who had been posted as lookout hurried up, pointing skyward. "Some kind of flying wagon coming!"

Retief and the others watched as a foreign-made heli settled in nearby. A small, undernourished-looking Voion with an oversized head lowered himself from the cockpit, unfurled a white flag, and approached, moving unsteadily on wheels several spokes of which were flapping loose.

"All right, let him come—and try to remember not to remove his head before he gets here," Retief cautioned.

"You are Tief-tief, the rebel commander?" the newcomer called in a curiously weak voice.

Retief looked the envoy over carefully, nodded.

"We, ah, admire your spirit," the Voion went on. "For that reason we are considering offering you a general amnesty . . ."

Retief waited.

"If, er, we could discuss the details in private . . . ?" the emissary proposed in a hoarse whisper.

Retief nodded to Jik-jik and Tupper. "Would you fellows mind stepping aside for a minute or two?"

"OK, Tief-tief—but keep both oculars on that customer; he look to me like a slick one." They moved off a few yards.

"Go ahead," Retief said. "What's your proposition?"

The Voion was staring at him; he made a dry rasping sound. "Forgive my mirth," he hissed. "I confess I came here to salvage what I could from a debacle—but that voice—those legs . . ." The Voion's tone changed to a confident rasp: "I have just revised my terms. You will relinquish command of this rabble at once and accompany me as a prisoner to Planetary Field HQ!"

"Why," Retief inquired interestedly, "would I do that?"

"For an excellent reason. In fact, for ten excellent reasons, my dear Retief!" The Voion reached to its head, fumbled—then lifted off a hollow headpiece to reveal a pale gray face and five inquisitive eye stalks.

"Well, General Hish of the Groaci Legation," Retief said. "You're out of your territory."

Hish fixed two pairs of eyes on Retief. "We have in our custody the person of ten Terry females, removed from a disabled vessel illegally on Voion soil," he said coldly. "They are scheduled to be shot at dawn. I offer you their lives in return for the surrender of yourself!"

6

"When you coming back, Tief-tief?" Jik-jik inquired worriedly. "How come you going off with this here policeman in this here apparatus?"

"I'll be back as soon as I can," Retief said. "Keep up the hit and run tactics—and recruit every tribe you meet."

"To get aboard," the disguised alien said in Groaci. "To make haste to arrive before the executions."

Retief stepped into the two-man heli in which the emissary had arrived. The latter strapped in, started up, lifted from the wheel-scarred field, then turned in the seat and cocked three unoccupied eyes at Retief. "I congratulate you on your wisdom' in coming along quietly," he whispered in excellent Terran. "I of course disapprove of bloodshed, but without the compelling argument which your presence at Planetary HQ will present, I fear my protests would never have availed to preserve intact the prisoners."

"You still haven't told me what a Groaci military man is doing out here in the brush, General—"

"Please—address me merely as Hish. My Voion associates know me only as a helpful adviser. If my voice is to be effective in securing clemency for the captives, no complicating new elements must be introduced into the present rather fragile equation."

"For a group enjoying the services of a high-powered military adviser," Retief said, "the Planetary Army shows a surprising ignorance of the elements of warfare."

"I've only just arrived in the field today," Hish said. "As for these native levies—hopeless. But no matter. In the absence of your restraining presence your irregulars will doubtless devise a suitable disposition for them. The survivors, if any, will perhaps have learned a lesson or two from the experience which will stand them in good stead during coming campaigns under my tutelage."

There was a heavy satchel on the floor by Retief's feet, its top gaping open. "I see you're taking a practical view of matters," Retief commented. He studied a dull-glinting shape inside the bag. "I confess I'm curious as to just what it is you Groaci expect to net from the operation." As he spoke, he reached casually, lifted out the inert form of a two-inch Quoppina, a harsh yellow in color, remarkably heavy. Beneath it, he saw another, similar trophy, this one a soft silvery color. He replaced the dead specimens.

"Shall we say—new customers . . .?" Hish whispered, staring ahead at the jungle below.

"The prospect of opening up a new market for your usual line of hardware isn't sufficient inducement to launch a hardheaded group like yourselves on a risky adventure under the collective CDT nose."

"Ah, but perhaps the new Planetary Government, sensible of the close ties binding them to the Groaci state, will spurn continued intervention in internal affairs by reactionary Terran influences . . ."

"Booting the Terries is part of the deal, eh? There's still something you're not being perfectly candid about, Hish. What's in it for the Groaci?"

"One must keep a few little secrets," Hish chided. "And now I must give my attention to landing; such an awkward business, laboring under the weight of this bulky disguise. Still, it's necessary; the rank and file of my associates seem to suffer from the sort of anti-foreign animus so typical of bucolics."

There were lights below, the dark rectangles of tents, the raw scars of hastily scraped camp streets, packed with the hurrying ant-shapes of Voion. To one side of the field headquarters, Retief saw a rank of parked Rhoon, unnaturally still as technicians crawled over them under the glare of portable polyarcs. The heli dropped in to a bumpy landing, was at once surrounded by Voion, nervously fingering weapons. Hish replaced his headpiece, opened the hatch and scrambled out. An officious-looking Voion staff officer bustled up, gave Retief a hostile look.

"Who's this, Hish-hish?" he demanded. "Their truce representative, I suppose?"

"By no means, Xic," Hish whispered in his weak Groaci voice. "Instruct your chaps to keep a sharp eye on this fellow; he's my prisoner."

"What do we want with more prisoners—and a Stilter at that? I've already suffered a number of nasty dents from the legs of those Terry cows you insisted we bring in—"

"Enough Xic; I've had a trying evening—"

"What did you manage in the way of truce terms? I suppose they're demanding outrageous reparations for those few trivial villages that accidentally caught on fire—"

"On the contrary, they demand nothing. I left them to their own devices. Now—'"

"What about our troops? Those rabble are holding an entire brigade of highly polished soldiers immobilized out there! Why, the cost of the inlays alone—"

"The fortunes of war, my dear Major. Now, if you please, I have important matters to discuss—"

"What's more important than salvaging my brigade?" the outraged officer shrilled. "How can I be adjutant of an organization that's been scrapped by the enemy?"

"A neat problem in administration, sir. Possibly if you carry them on your morning report as 'Missing in Action' . . ."

"Hmmm. That might work—at least until next payday. Meanwhile, why not disassemble this Stilter and get on with planning our next victory?"

"This Stilter will play an important part in that happy event, Xic. He happens to be the rebel commander."

"Him?" Xic canted his oculars alertly at Retief. "How in Quopp did you manage to capture him?"

"I have a certain skill in these matters. Bring him along now to my tent—"

"Not until the prisoners are released," Retief said. "I want to see them put aboard a couple of helis and on their way."

"What's this? A prisoner dictating terms?" Xic keened.

"No matter; the wenches have served their purpose. I had in mind ransoming them off for concessions from the Terry ambassador, but the present arrangement has a certain euphony. Go along to the stockade and see that they're released at once."

"I'll go with you," Retief said.

"You'll do as you're ordered!" Major Xic snapped. "Or I'll shorten those stilts of your by a joint to bring you down to a more manageable size!"

"No, you won't. You'll carefully keep me intact and reasonably well pleased with things. Hish-hish would like it that way."

"We'll indulge his fancy for the moment, Major," the Groaci hissed. "Kindly lead the way."

The Voion clacked his palps angrily and rolled off toward a stoutly palisaded enclosure looming above the lines of low tents along the company streets. At a heavy gate made of stout logs welded together, a guard produced a foot-long key, opened a huge padlock, hauled the portal wide, then shouted to a compatriot above. Lights sprang on at the corner towers. Xic motioned a squad of Voion through, then followed, Hish close on his heels, Retief and an additional squad behind him.

There was an outcry ahead. Four Voion shrilled simultaneously, an effect not unlike the vocalizations of mating cats, though magnified. The Voion around Retief jerked up their clubs. Hish darted ahead. Retief pushed after him, came up beside the Voion officer who was waving all four arms and swiveling his oculars excitedly while the soldiers peered about the thirty-yard square enclosure, all explaining at once.

"Where are the Terrans?" Hish whispered. "What have you done with my prisoners?"

"Quiet!" the major shrieked. He turned to Hish, assuming a nonchalant angle of the antennae.

"Too bad, Hish-hish," he said airily. "It appears they've excavated a tunnel and departed."

"It was the one with the copper-colored cranial filaments!" a guard explained. "It demanded digging tools so that it and its fellow could eplivate the ratesifrans . . ."

"What's that?" Hish demanded.

"I don't know!" the major yelled. "Something to do with a tribal taboo; and if you think my boys are going to call down the wrath of the Worm—"

"Beware . . . lest you call down a more immediate ill temper," Hish snarled. He calmed himself with a visible effort, turned on Retief. "An unexpected development—but the females appear to be free, just as you desired—"

"Not exactly," Retief cut him off. "I desired to see them turned loose with a fighting chance of getting across a hundred miles of jungle and back to Ixix."

"Ah, well, life is filled with these trifling disappointments, my dear Retief. Suppose we go along to my tent now and proceed with business . . ."

"Thanks, but I won't be able to make it," Retief said affably. "I have to be getting back to the wars."

"Be realistic, Retief," Hish urged. "My end of the bargain was fulfilled in a rather informal manner, true, but surely you are not so naive as to imagine that detail nullifies the spirit of our agreement . . .?"

Retief glanced at the looming stockade walls, the Voion ringing him in. "What spirit would that be?"

"One of cooperation," Hish purred. "I suggest we move along from these depressing surroudings now and conduct our little chat in more comfortable circumstances—"

"I'm afraid you've gotten a couple of false impressions along the line somewhere," Retief said. "I just agreed to come with you; I didn't promise to do your homework for you."

"Surely the supplying of certain information was implicit in your surrender!"

"Why natter with the scoundrel?" the Voion major put in. "I have specialists on my staff who'll put him into a talking mood!"

"Don't be tiresome, Retief," Hish whispered. "I can squeeze the truth out of you; but why force me to these uncouth tactics?"

"Oh, maybe I have an idea you don't know just where I stand, and that you're a little reluctant to damage CDT property—"

"What's he talking about?" the Voion demanded. "What has this to do with interloping Terries?"

"Silence!" Hish snapped. "Go busy yourself with executing the slackers responsible for the escape, or some other routine task—"

"Who do you think you're talking to?" the major keened. "Some headquarters goldbrick sent you out here to poke around and count paper clips, but if you think you can talk that way to me and get away with it—"

"Calm yourself, Major! I should dislike to employ my influence with Prime Minister Ikk to have you transferred to duty on—certain other fronts . . ." Hish turned back to Retief. "You will now give me full particulars on rebel troop concentrations, or suffer the consequences!"

"Suppose we just jump directly along to the consequences," Retief proposed. "It will save time all around."

"As you will, then." Hish turned back to Xic. "Since your stockade has proven inadequate to requirements, what other facilities can you offer for the restraint of the prisoner?"

"Well—there's a nice little room behind post headquarters, specially built to house the officers' stimulant supply—if we ever get any. If it's good enough to keep my kleptomaniacs out of the Hellrose, it ought to keep this Stilter in."

"Very well," Hish snapped. "Take him there and chain him to the wall.

The cell was a cramped, low-ceilinged chamber with damp mud walls retained by log pilings only the upper foot of which were above ground level; through the narrow openings between uprights, Retief could see the muddy polyarc-lit acres of the camp stretching a hundred yards to the nearest jungle perimeter. The crowd of Voion who had escorted him there crowded in, watching as the head jailor shook out a length of tough chain, welded one end to a projecting stub on an ironwood corner post, then approached Retief.

"Just sit quiet now, Stilter," he ordered, "while I throw a loop around your neck—and no backchat, or I'll weld your mandibles shut."

"How about putting it on my left stilt instead," Retief proposed. "That way it won't interfere with my thinking nice thoughts about you, just in case my side wins."

"Confidentially," the welder said in a low voice. "Just how strong *are* you boys?"

"Well, let's see," Retief considered. "There are five billion Quoppina on Quopp; subtract two million Voion, and that leaves—"

"Wow!" a gaping guard said. "That's better'n two to one, pretty near—"

"Shut up, Vop!" the warder buzzed. "Stick out that stilt, Stilter!' Retief complied, watched as the Voion threw two loops of stout chain around his ankle, welded the links together.

"That ought to hold you until Hish-hish gets through arguing with the major and comes down to work you over. The Voion snapped off his portable welder. "If you need anything, just yell. The exercise'll do you good."

"What time is breakfast served?" Retief inquired.

"Oh, I'll throw a couple slabs of over-aged Dink in to you after a while—if I think of it." The guards filed from the cell, taking their torches with them, the warder bringing up the rear. He looked back from the door.

"That bad?" he queried. "Five billion of youse?"

"Worse," Retief agreed solemnly. "Some of us vote twice."

There was silence after the door clanked shut. Along the narrow gap between the top of the excavation and the sagging log ceiling half a dozen inquisitive Voion faces were ducked down, staring in at the dark pit; they saw nothing, tired of the sport, rolled off to other pastimes. Retief picked a relatively dry spot, sat down, quickly unsnapped the leather soled foot-covering from his chained leg, pulled off the shoe, then unbuckled the greavelike shin armor, worked it out from under the loops. A moment later his leg was free. He resumed the leg- and foot-pieces, shook out the chain and arranged a slip noose for use in the event of sudden callers, then scouted the small room. The metallo-wood posts were deep-set, six inches apart. He chipped at one with the clawed gauntlet on his right hand; it was like scratching at a fireplug. The air space above the wall was hardly more promising; the clearance under the ceiling was no more than eight inches, and the gap between verticals hardly a foot . . .

A movement beyond the barrier caught Retief's eye; a pattern of glowing, greenish dots danced in the air a few yards distant, bobbed, came closer.

"Tief-tief!" a tiny voice peeped. "Tief-tief caught-caught!"

"Well—you know my name." Something small and bright green buzzed through the opening, hovering on three-inch rotors.

"Save-save George-George," the tiny flyer said. "Tief-tief pal-pal!"

Retief held out his hand. The six-inch Quoppina—a Phip—settled on it, perched like a jeweled ornament, its head a deep green, its short body a brilliant chartreuse with forest green stripes, its four straw-thin legs a bright sunshine yellow.

"Phip-phip help-help," it stated in its tiny voice.

"That's a very friendly offer," Retief said. "There might be something you could do, at that. How about rounding up a couple of your friends and see if you can find a few things for me . . ."

Retief studied the six-foot-long, two-foot-deep trench he had scooped in the stiff clay of the cell floor, rimmed on one side by a low parapet heaped up from the excavated material.

"That will have to do," he said to the half dozen Phips who perched along the sill, watching the proceedings. "Old Hish will be hotfooting it down here any time now to see if durance vile has softened me up."

A last flight of Phips buzzed in through the wall openings, deposited their bean-sized contributions in the small heaps laid out on a mat of leaves flown in for the purpose.

"All-all," one hummed. "Gone-gone."

"That's all right," Retief assured the small creature. "I've got enough now." He lifted a wide leaf heaped with shreaded bark selected by the Phips for its high cellulose content, placed it atop the heaped-earth revetment beside the foxhole. "Somebody give me a light," he called. A Phip settled in, struck its rear legs together with a sound like a file on glass. At the third try a spark jumped. Retief blew gently on it, watched as the fuel glowed, burst into a bright green flame. He covered the small blaze with another broad leaf; yellowish smoke boiled out. He held the damper in place until the low-oxygen combustion was complete, then lifted it to reveal a double handful of black residue.

"That ought to do the job; now let's prepare the rest of the ingredients."

He picked up a rough-surfaced slab of ironwood previously split off a post, began grating sourballs into a fine powder.

Half an hour later, Retief packed the last pinch of the finely divided mixture into the container he had improvised from nicklewood leaves, carefully wrapped with lengths of tough wire-vine. He crimped down the top, inserted a fuse made from a strip of shirt-sleeve impregnated with the home-made gunpowder.

"Now, when I give the word, light it off," he instructed the hovering Phips. "Just one of you; the rest will have to stand back at a good distance. And as soon as it's lit—head for the tall timber, fast! Don't wait around to see what happens."

"Kay-kay, Tief-Tief," a Phip chirped. "Now-now?"

"In just a minute . . ." He hefted the bomb. "A good pound and a half; that ought to have a salutary effect." He placed the rude package on the ledge against an upright, pressed it firmly in position, then packed clay around it, leaving the fuse clear.

"That's it," he said. He stepped into the trench, settled himself face-down.

"Light it off, fellows—and don't forget to hightail it . . ."

There was the busy humming of small rotors, then a harsh rasping as the selected Phip struck a spark. A brief sputtering followed, accompanied by the hasty whine of the departing Phip, then silence. Retief waited. He sniffed. Was there a faint odor of burning rag . . . ?

The *boom!* lifted Retief bodily, slammed him back against the floor of his retreat under an avalanche of mud and screaming wood fragments. He thrust himself clear, spat dirt, his head ringing like a giant gong. There was a harsh stink of chemicals, a taste in his mouth like charred sneakers. Cool air blew from a gaping cavern where the wall had been. A timber sagged from above; beyond it he could see smoke swirling in a room littered with shattered lumber.

A Phip buzzed close. "Fun-fun," it shrilled. "Gain-gain!"

"Some other time," Retief said blurrily. "And remind me to use smaller amounts . . ." He ducked under the fallen ceiling beams, went up the blast-gouged slope, emerged into the open. Voion shot past him, inaudible in the shrill ringing in Retief's ears. Out of the smoke haze, the slight figure of General Hish appeared, arms waving. Retief straight-armed the Groaci, saw him go end over end, one artificial wheel bouncing free to go rolling off into the brush. He sprinted, dodged a pair of Voion who belatedly skittered into his path, plunged into the dark wall of the jungle.

7

The trail left by the fleeing prisoners was not difficult to follow; bits of lacy cloth, dropped hankies, candy wrappers, and the deep prints of spike heels served to indicate their direction of flight as plainly as a set of hand-painted signposts. The girls had pushed through dense thickets for a hundred yards, then encountered a well-defined trail leading in an approximately westward direction. It was now after Second Jooprise, and Retief moved along in multicolored gloom beneath towering trees of a thousand varieties, each bearing metal-bright leaves in gay tones, which rustled and tinkled, clashing with soft musical notes as the arching branches stirred to the wind.

Half an hour's walk brought him to a stream of clear water bubbling over a shallow, sandy bottom bright with vivid-colored pebbles. Small aquatic Quoppina the size of Phips darted to and fro in the sun-dappled water, propelled by rotating members modified by evolutionary processes into twin screws astern.

The water looked tempting. Retief hung his sword on a convenient branch, lifted off the helmet he had been wearing for the past eighteen hours, unstrapped the leather side-buckles and shed the chest and back armor, then splashed into the stream and dashed cold water over his face and arms. Back on shore, he settled himself under a mauve-barked tree, took out one of the concentrated food bars Ibbl had provided.

From above, a plaintive keening sounded. Retief looked up into the tree, saw something move in the Jooplight, striking down through branches and glittering dark foliage—a flash of vivid purple among the blackish-red leaves. There was a second movement, lower down. Retief made out the almost invisible form of a wiry, slender Quoppina, gorgeous violet where the light struck him, decorated with white-edged purple rosettes, a perfect camouflage in the light-mottled foliage. The creature hung motionless, wailing softly.

Retief jumped, caught a branch, pulled himself up, then climbed higher, avoiding the knife-edged leaves. From a position astride a stout limb twenty feet up, he could make out the cleverly concealed lines of a narrow-mesh net in which the captive—a Flink, Retief saw—hung, a tangle of purple limbs, twisted ropes, and anxiously canted oculars.

"What happened, fellow? Pull the wrong string and catch yourself?"

"I'm laughing," the Flink said glumly, in a high, thin voice.

"So go ahead, gloat," a second Flink voice called from above. "Rub it in."

"Just a minute and I'll cut you down," Retief offered.

"Hey, me first," the upper Flink called. "It was him started the trouble, remember? Me, I'm a peaceful Flink, bothering nobody—"

"It's a different Stilter, you lowlife," the nearer Flink called hastily. "This ain't the one from before."

"Oh, you've seen other Stilters around?" Retief inquired interestedly.

"Maybe; you know how it is. You meet all kinds of people."

"You're not being completely candid, I'm afraid. Come on—give."

"Look," the Flink said. "Such a crick I've got: How about cutting me down first and we'll chat after?"

"*He's* got a crick," the other Flink shrilled hoarsely.

"Ha! In *his* lousy net I'm hanging! Six cricks I've got, all worse than his!"

"You think this noose is maybe comfortable?" the first came back hotly. "Rope burns I'm getting—"

"Let's compare notes later," Retief interrupted. "Which way did the Stilters go?"

"You look like a nice, kind sort of Stilter," the nearest Flink said, holding his oculars on Retief as he swung in a gentle arc past him. "Let me down and I'll try to help you out with your problem. I mean, in such a position, who could talk?"

"Cut him down, and he's gone like a flash," the other called. "Now, I happen to like your looks, so I'll tell you what I'll do—"

"Don't listen," the roped Flink said in a confidential tone. "Look at him—and he claims to be number one tribal woodsman, yet. Some woodsman!"

"A woodsman like you I shouldn't be, even without you was hanging in my noose," the other countered. "Take it from me, Stilter, Ozzle's the biggest liar in the tribe, and believe me, competition he's got!"

"Fellows, I'm afraid I can't stay for a conference after all," Retief cut in. "Sorry to leave you hanging around in bad company, but—"

"Hold it!" the Flink called Ozzl screeched. "I've thought it over and I've decided: A nice fellow like you I want my family to meet—"

"Don't trust him! I'll tell you what: Get me out of this lousy rope, and I'm your Flink—"

"You expect this Stilter—such a fine-looking Quopp—he should believe that? As soon as I'm loose, everything I own is his!"

"So what'll he do with a pile of empties? My deal is better, believe me, Mister; you and me, such a talk we'll have, you wouldn't believe—"

"You're right; he wouldn't. Him and me, together a long chat we'll have—"

There was a flash of green, a sharp humming; the Phip was back, hovering before Retief's face.

"Tief-tief flip-flip," it churped. "Flip-flip Flink-flink!"

"Don't listen!" Ozzl screeched. "What does this midget know?"

"Flip-flip Flink-flink!" the Phip repeated.

"Hmmm. I seem to remember hearing somewhere that a Flink's word is good as long as he's standing on his head," Retief mused. "Thanks, partner." He gripped Ozzl's lower arms—in his species specialized as landing gear—and inverted the captive tree-dweller.

"If I cut you down, will you tell me where the Stilters are?"

"OK, OK, you got me," the Flink chirped glumly. "Cut me down and the whole miserable story I'll give you."

Retief extracted a similar promise from the second Flink.

"Look out, now," the latter cautioned. "All around is nets."

Retief made out the cleverly concealed lines of other nets and nooses, some small, some large enough to gather in a fair-sized Quoppina.

"Thanks for the warning," Retief said. "I might have walked right in to one of those."

Five minutes later both captives had been lowered to the ground and cut free. They sprawled, groaning, working their arms and experimentally revving up their rotation members: small pulleylike wheels which they customarily hooked over vines or branches for fast travel.

"Well," Ozzl sighed. "Me and Nopl, first class trappers we're supposed to be. Such a picture, the two of us in our own ropes hung up!"

"Nothing's busted," Nopl said. "Boy, such a experience!"

"Don't stall, gentlemen," Retief said. "The time has come to tell all: Where did you see the Stilters, how long ago, and which way did they go when they left?"

"A promise is a promise—but listen—you won't tell, OK?"

"I won't tell."

Ozzl sighed. "All right. It was this way . . ."

". . . so I turn around, and zzzskttt! The Stilter with the copper-colored head filaments—the one the others called Fi-fi—pulls the trip wire—such a dummy I was to explain it—and there I am, downside up. It was humiliating!"

"Under the circumstances, a little humility seems appropriate," Retief suggested. "And after the Stilter tricked you into your own net, what then?"

"Then the two-timer cuts down the rest of the Stilters, and off they go—thataway." Ozzl pointed.

"Yeah," the other Flink said aggrievedly. "So there we hung until you come along—and all because we try to be polite and show that Stilter how the nets work, such an interest it was expressing."

Retief nodded sympathetically. "We Stilters are a tricky lot, especially when anybody tries to violate our tribal taboo against being eaten. And on that note I must leave you—"

"What's the rush?" Ozzl demanded. "Stick around awhile; a little philosophy we'll kick around."

"What about a drink, fellows?" Ozzl proposed. He took a hip flask from the flat pouch strapped to his lean flank, quaffed deeply, rose to his full three foot six, flexed his arms. "A new Quopp that'll make out of you," he announced and passed the bottle to Retief. He took a swallow; like all Quoppina liquors, it was thin, delicately flavored, resembling dilute honey. He passed the flask to Nopl, who drank, offered sulphurous sourballs which Retief declined.

"They're a good two hours ahead of me," he said. "I have to make up some time—"

The Phip was back, buzzing around Retief's head.

"Tief-tief," the Phip hummed. "Nip-nip!"

"Sure, give the little stool pigeon a shot," Nopl offered. "Whoopee! Life is just a bowl of snik-berries!"

"My pal, Tief-tief!" Ozzl slung one long, pulley-wheeled member across the lower portion of Retief's back in comradely fashion. "You're a shrewd dealer for a . . . a . . . whatever kind Quoppina you are!"

Nopl took another pull at the flask. "Tief-tief, you should meet the crowd," he shrilled cheerfully. "A swell bunch, am I right, Ozzl?"

"Such a swell bunch, I'm crying," the Flink replied. "When I think what a swell bunch they are I wonder, what did I do to deserve it?"

"They're a lousy crowd teetotaling small-timers, but so what?" Nopl caroled. "Tief-tief they should meet."

"Sorry," Retief said. "Some other time."

Ozzl made a noise like a broken connecting rod, the Flink expression of suppressed merriment. "Guess again,

Tief-tief," he caroled, and waved a wheeled member in an all-encompassing gesture. "Meet the boys!"

Retief glanced upward. From behind every leafy branch and vine-shrouded shrub, a purple Quoppina materialized, a rope or net in hand, a few nocking arrows to small bows, one or two armed with long, flexible tridents.

"About time," Nopl said and hiccuped. "I thought you boys would never show."

Retief stood in the center of the patch of open, Jooplit sward beneath the big tree from which a hundred silent Flink hung like grotesque fruits. An overweight Flink with the wine-purple carapace of mature age tilted myopic oculars at him. "These two loafers I send out, they should check the traps and with a drinking buddy they come reeling back," he commented bitterly.

"Who's reeling? Am I reeling? Look at me," Ozzl invited.

"What about the Stilter?" someone called. "He looks like prime stock—with a cheese sauce, maybe he should be served—

"My pal, Tief-tief, nobody cuts up! First I'll drop dead!"

"This I could arrange," the oldster cut him off. "Now, if we slice up this Stilter, a snack for everybody he'll make—"

"Stop right there," Nopl shrilled. "A businessman like Tief-tief we couldn't eat! Cannibalism, yet, it would be! Instead, we'll truss him up and sell him—or maybe disassemble him for spares . . ."

Cries rang back and forth as the Flink discussed the various proposals.

"Such a head I've got," Nopl groaned during a momentary lull. "I think I need another little snort."

"That booze of yours works fast," Retief commented. "You got through the buzz and into the hangover stage in record time."

"Hung over or no, Ozzl and me will stick by you, Tief-tief. If they vote to sell you, I'll put in a good word we should hold out for top price."

"Marked down you'll not be while I'm around," Ozzl agreed.

The elderly Flink emitted a shrill cry for silence. "The pros and cons we've discussed," they announced. "It looks like the cons have it." A rustle ran through the Flink ranks. The encircling tribesmen moved in closer, shaking out nets and ropes as they maneuvered for favorable positions, Retief drew his sword, stepped back against the nearest tree trunk.

"Hey," the oldster called. "What's that sharp thing? It looks dangerous! Put it away like a nice piece merchandise before somebody gets hurt."

"It's an old tribal custom among us Stilters that we make owning us as expensive as possible," Retief explained. "Who's going to be first to open an account?"

"It figures," the elder said judiciously. "Price supports, yet."

"Still, we try to be reasonable," Retief amplified. "I doubt if I'll disassemble more than a dozen Flink before you get a rope on me."

"Six," the Flink said flatly. "That's my top offer."

"I'm afraid we're not going to be able to get together," Retief said. "Maybe we'd better call off the whole deal."

"He's right," someone stated. "Worth twelve Flink, including maybe me, he's not."

Retief started forward, swinging the sword loosely. "Just step back, gentlemen," he suggested. "I have important business to transact, and no time to continue this delightful discussion—"

A noose whirled at him; he spun, slashed; the severed line dropped to the ground.

"Hey! That's expensive rope you're cutting," someone protested, hauling in the damaged lariat.

"Let him go," another suggested. "My rope I ain't risking."

"What's that?" the elder shrilled. "You want I should let valuable merchandise go stilting right out of sight?"

"Listen, Tief-tief," Ozzl called. "There's only the one trail, and it leads straight to the rock spire. Now, with us, you get sold for parts, so OK, there you are. But you climb up there and a Rhoon picks you up and flies off—I'm asking: Where are you?"

"Did you say Rhoon?" Retief inquired.

"On top of the rock spire they're thick like Phips on a jelly flower. A chance you haven't got!"

"Still, I think I'll risk it," Retief said. He moved toward the trail and two Flink rushed in, nets ready; he knocked them spinning, dodged two nets and a lasso, leaped for the dark tunnel of the trail and ran for it with a horde of Flink baying in hot puruist.

Later, on a rocky slope a hundred yards above the tops of the thick jungle growth below, Retief pulled himself up onto a flat boulder, turned and looked down at the Flink tribe clustered below, staring up and shaking fists.

"Dirty pool, Tief-tief," Ozzl yelled. "This kind terrain, our wheels ain't meant for."

"Thanks for escorting me this far," Retief called. "I'll find my way from here."

"Sure." The Flink waved a member at the steep escarpments rising above. "Just keep climbing. The Rhoon roost is only about a mile—straight up. If you don't fall off and get killed, the Rhoon you'll find after a while—or they'll find you." He clicked his antennae in the Gesture of Sentimental Farewell. "You were a good drinking buddy, Tief-tief. Hang loose."

Retief scanned the slope above; he had a stiff climb ahead. He lifted off his helmet, pulled off the gauntlets, slung them by a thong to his belt. He shook his canteen; nearly empty. He took a last look at the valley and started up the almost vertical slope.

It was an hour after dawn when Retief reached a narrow ledge a thousand feet above the jungle valley below. The wind whistled here, unimpeded by Quoppian flora; in the distance, a pair of white flyers of medium size wheeled and dipped under the ominous sky of approaching First Eclipse, where the fire-edged disk of Joop rushed to its rendezvous with the glaring Quopp sun. Far above, a mere spec in the dark blue sky, a lone Rhoon circled the towering peak where the giant flyers nested.

Retief studied the rock face above; it was a smooth expanse of black slatelike stone rising sheer from the ledge. The route upward, it appeared, ended here.

One of the white aerialists was dropping lower, coming in to look over the intruder. Retief donned his headpiece, shifted his sword hilt to a convenient angle, waited for the visitor. He could hear the beat of its rotors now, see the pale coral markings along the underside of the body, the black legs folded against the chest region, the inquisitive oculars canted to look him over.

"What seek you here upon the wind slopes, groundling?" a thin voice called down to him, tattered by the gusty breeze. "There's naught for your kind here but unforgiving rock spires and the deep, cold air."

"They say the Rhoon have their nests up there," Retief called.

"That do they—up a-high, where low clouds scrape their bellies and death blooms grow amid the moss as black as night." The flying creature dropped closer; the slipstream from its ten-foot rotors battered at Retief, whirling dust into his face. He gripped the rock, braced his feet apart.

"Aiiii!" the flyer called. "If a zephyr from my passing can come nigh to spill you from your perch, how will you fare when some great lordling of the Rhoon comes like a cyclone to attend you here?"

"I'll work on that one when I get to it," Retief shouted over the tumult.

"If you've come to steal my eggs, you've picked a lonely death."

"Is there any other kind?"

The flyer settled lower, reached out and gripped a buttress of rock with black talons; its rotors whined to a stop.

"Perhaps you've tired of life, chained to the world, and you've come here to launch yourself into one glorious taste of flight," it hazarded.

"Just paying a social call," Retief assured the creature. "But I seem to have run out of highway. You wouldn't happen to know an easier route up?"

"A social call? I see you wish a braver death than a mere tumble to the rocks."

"I'd like to sample the view from the top; I hear it's very impressive."

"The view of raging Rhoonhood stooping to defend a nest is said to be the fearsomest on Quopp," the flyer agreed. "However, few eyewitness tales of the experience are told."

Retief studied the creature's rotors, spinning slowly as the wind sighed over the thin, curved blades.

"How much weight can you lift?" he inquired.

"I once plucked up a full-grown Flink and dropped him in the river, yonder," the flyer motioned with one limber arm. "I doubt if he'll come thieving 'round my nest again."

"I weigh more than a Flink," Retief pointed out.

"No matter that: You'd fall as fast as any Flink, and make a better splash."

"I'll bet you can't lift me," Retief challenged. The flyer revved its rotors, shifting its grip on its perch.

"Most groundlings plead for life when once I catch them on the rock spires. Now you invite my wrath."

"Oh no, I'm just talking about flying me up there." Retief pointed to the peaks towering above.

"Fly you . . . ?"

"Sure. I can't walk up a vertical wall, and it wouldn't be convenient to go down and look for another route."

"Can you be serious, poor earthbound grub? Would you indeed trust life and limb to me?"

"Most Quoppina will keep their word to a harmless stranger. Why should you be any different?"

"A curious rationale," the flyer said, "and yet, withal, a most refreshing one. I'd come to think of crawlers all as timid things, who cling and whimper out their fear when I come on them here among the lonely peaks. And now here's one who speaks as boldly as a flyer born!"

"Just put me down anywhere in climbing range of Rhoon country," Retief suggested.

"A strange anomaly is this: A wingless one who dares to come among the masters of the sky!" The flyer whirled its rotors, lifted, drifted, hovering, toward Retief. "I'll put you to the test then, groundling! Perhaps you'll weight me down, and then together we'll go tumbling toward our death below. But if my rotors hold, I'll bear you up, my life upon it!"

"Fair enough." Retief sheathed his sword, squinting against the down-blast of air. He reached for the steel-hard grapples of the flyer, gripped, held on. Air screamed as the whirling blades raced, biting for purchase; then he was lifting, floating up, wind screaming past his face, the mountainside dwindling away below.

The flying creature rose swiftly for a hundred feet; then it slowed, gained another fifty feet, inched upward, its rotors laboring now. A gust of wind tilted it, and it dropped, then righted itself, struggled upward again, paralleling the smooth face of rock at a distance of thirty feet, Retief estimated. A small white flower growing from a crevice caught his eye; slowly it dropped below him as the flyer gained altitude foot by foot. Above, Retief could see a tiny ledge where the vertical face ended, and above it a long sweep, only slightly less steep, to a lone spire thrusting up another five hundred feet against the darkening sky.

"How say you, groundling?" the laboring flyer's voice rang out, "will you trust me to press on, or shall I give it up and place you safe below?"

"Just a little way now,' Retief called. "You can do it, old timer."

"I like the groundling's spirit, wings or no!" the Quoppina shouted into the wind. "We'll hazard all . . . and win or die . . . and none can say we quailed before the test!"

"You'd better save your wind for flying," Retief called. "We'll stage a self-congratulation session after we get there."

The wind whipped, buffeting. The cliff face moved past with agonizing sloth. Retief's hands were numb from the strain; the ledge was still twenty feet above, inching closer. The Quoppina's breathing was loud, wheezing; the sound of the rotors had changed timbre. They seemed to flutter now, as though the blades were loose. Then another sound was audible—a sharp whirring, coming closer. . . .

Retief twisted his head. A second flying Quoppina had come up from the port beam; it hovered, studying the situation with alert oculars.

"That one's too big to eat, Gulinda!" it called. "I'll wager he's as tough as Wumblum wheel rim!"

"I'll place him . . . safe above . . . or die . . ." Retief's flyer got out.

"Ah—then it's a wager! Well, I suggest you waste no time. A Rhoon has seen you now, and half a minute hence he'll be here."

Retief's flyer grunted a reply, settled down to steady pulling. Ten feet more, five, three . . .

There was a deep thrumming, a beat of wind that bounced the flyer closer to the cliff face. Retief craned, saw the huge-bodied shape of a fast-descending Rhoon silhouetted against the vast, glittering disks of its spinning rotors. With a final, gear-screeching effort, the smaller flyer surged upward the final yard, banked toward the ledge. "Farewell! it screamed. Retief dropped, slammed stony ground, fetched up against the rising wall above as the Rhoon pounced, hissing, its fanged eating jaws wide. Retief rolled away as the Rhoon struck out with a barbed hind leg, missed and struck again, sent stone chips flying. A narrow crevice split the rock a yard distant; Retief dived for it, wedged himself in just as the disk of Joop cut off the blackish sunlight like a snapped switch. Long Rhoon talons raked against the rock, sending a shower of bright sparks glimmering against the sudden dark. Then, with a hoarse scream, the Rhoon lifted away; the beat of its rotors faded. Retief leaned back in his cramped refuge, let out his breath with a long sigh, alone now with the stars that twinkled in the false night of the eclipse and the moaning wind that searched among the rock crannies.

Retief rested while Joop edged across the bright corona of the distant sun; the glowing halo bulged, then burst into full light as the transit was completed. He scanned the sky; a pair of Rhoon circled far above, light flicking from their rotors. He squeezed out of his hideaway, looked over the edge of the two-foot shelf on which he stood. Far below, the ledge from which he had hitched the ride to his present position showed as a thin line against vertical rock—and far below that, the jungle stretched like a varicolored carpet across low hills to distant haze.

He looked up; striated rock loomed, topped by a rock spire that thrust up like a knife blade a final hundred feet. Retief turned back to the cranny in which he had hidden. It narrowed sharply into darkness—but a steady flow of cold air funneled from it. He went to hands and knees, pushed through the first narrowing, found that the passage widened slightly. Above, the sky was a bright blue line between the rising walls of rock. He rose, crunching brittle debris underfoot, braced his back against one face of the chimney, started upward.

Halfway up, Retief found an outthrust shoulder of rock on which to rest. He ate half a food bar, took a swallow of water—the last in his canteen. Then he went on.

Once the cleft narrowed, then widened out into a near-cave, from which a cloud of tiny gray-black Quoppina no bigger than hummingbirds swarmed in alarm, battering at his face, uttering supersonic cries. Again, the black shadow of a Rhoon swept across the strip of sky above, momentarily blacking out the meager light. The armor chafed, cutting into his back; his hands were cut in a dozen places from the sharp-edged rock.

The crevasse widened again ten feet from the top. Retief made the last few yards in a scramble up a deeply scored slope half-choked with weathered and faded fragments of Quoppina exoskeleton and sun-bleached organic gears looped by tangles of corroded internal wiring. The Rhoon, it appeared, were messy eaters.

Keeping in black shadow, Retief studied the open sky; a thousand feet above, two Rhoon wheeled lazily, unaware of the intruder in their domain. He stood, dusted himself off, looked around at an oval platform fifteen by twenty feet, backed at one side by a spear of rock that rose ten feet to a needle point, edged on the remainder of its periphery by a void that yawned across to a stupendous view of high, lonely peaks, only a few of which topped his present vantage point. Closer at hand, a heap of round boulders caught his eye: Butter-yellow spheres eighteen inches in diameter. He went to them, tapped the smooth surface of one; it gave off a hollow, metallic bong. There were six of them—Rhoon eggs, piled here to hatch in the sun.

Retief glanced toward the monster parents circling above, still apparently serenely ignorant of his presence.

The big eggs were heavy, unwieldy in their lopsidedness. He lifted down the topmost spheroid, rolled it across to the cliff's edge, propped it, delicately poised, just above the brink. The next two eggs he ranged beside the first. Two more eggs formed a short second rank, with the final orb positioned atop the others. Retief dusted his hands, resumed the helmet and gauntlets he had laid aside earlier, then posted himself squarely before the gargantuan Easter display and settled down to wait.

8

A cold wind whipped down from the deep blue sky. Retief watched the mighty Rhoon elders wheeling in the distance, tireless as the wind—a description which, he reflected, did not apply equally to himself.

Half an hour passed. Retief watched the high white clouds that marched past like gunboats hurrying to distant battles. He shifted to a more comfortable position leaning against a convenient boulder, closed his eyes against the brightness of the sky. . . .

A rhythmic, thudding whistle brought him suddenly wide awake. A hundred feet above, an immense Rhoon swelled visibly as it dropped to the attack, its giant rotors hammering a tornado of air down at him, swirling up dust in a choking cloud. The Rhoon's four legs were extended, the three-foot-long slashing talons glinting like blue steel in the sunlight, the open biting jaws looking wide enough to swallow an ambassador at one gulp.

Retief braced himself, both hands on the topmost of the pyramid of eggs as the flying behemoth darkened the sun—

At the last possible instant the Rhoon veered off, shot past the peak like a runaway airliner, leaving a thin shriek trailing in the air behind it. Retief turned, saw it mount up into view again, its thirty-foot propellers flexing under the massive acceleration pressures. It swung in to hover scant yards away.

"Who comes to steal Gerthudion's eggs?" the great creature screamed.

"I want a word with you," Retief called. "The egg arrangement is just a conversation piece."

"High have you crept to reach my nest, and slow was your progress," the Rhoon steam-whistled. "I promise you a quicker return passage!" It edged closer, rocking in the gusty wind.

"Careful with that draft," Retief cautioned. "I feel a sneeze coming on; I'd hate to accidentally nudge your future family over the edge."

"Stand back, egg-napper! If even one of my darlings falls. I'll impale you on a rock spike to dry in the sun!"

"I propose a truce; you restrain your violent impulses and I'll see to it no accidents happen to the eggs."

"You threaten me, impudent mite? You'd bribe me with my own precious Rhoonlets?"

"I sincerely hope so. If you'll just perch somewhere, I'll tell you what it's all about."

"Some reason must there be for such madness under the morning sun! To hear the why of it, I confess I'm curious!" The Rhoon mother swung across the platform, settled in at the far edge in a flurry of dust, clinging to the rock with four jointed legs like lengths of polished gray pipe. Her yard-long head reared up a full fifteen feet to stare down at Retief, the shadows of her rotors flicking across her horny features as the blades slowed to a leisurely wind-driven twirl.

"Mind you don't twitch, now, and send what remains of your short future tumbling down into the abyss," the huge flyer admonished in a voice that boomed like a pipe organ. "Now, tell me: Why chose you this peculiar means of dying?"

"Dying isn't exactly what I had in mind," Retief corrected. "I'm looking for a party of Terrans—Stilters, somewhat like me, you know—and—"

"And you think to find them here?"

"Not exactly; but I have an idea you can help me find them."

"I, Gerthudion, lend aid to the trivial enterprises of a planet-bound mite? The thin air of the steps has addled your wits!"

"Still, I predict you'll take an interest before long."

The Rhoon edged closer, stretching its neck. "Your time grows short, daft groundling," she rumbled. "Now tell me what prompts you to dare such insolence!"

"I don't suppose you've been following recent political developments down below?" Retief hazarded.

"What cares Gerthudion for such?" the Rhoon boomed. "Wide are the skies and long the thoughts of the Rhoon-folk—"

"Uh-huh. I'm a long-thought fan myself," Retief put in. "However, a brand of mite called the Voion have been cutting a lot of people's thinking off short lately—"

"How could any petty dirt-creeper cut short the thoughts of a free-born Rhoon?"

"I'll get to that in a minute," Retief promised. "Is it true that you Rhoon have keen eyesight . . .?"

"Keen is our vision, and long our gaze—"

"And your wind's not bad, either. Too bad you're too big for a career in diplomacy; you could keep a round of peace talks going for a record run. Now, tell me, Gertie, have you noticed the smoke columns rising from the forest over there to the north?"

"That I have," the Rhoon snapped. "And lucky for you my eggs you're embracing, else I'd tumble you over the edge for your impertinence!"

"Those are tribal villages burning. The Voion are setting out to take over the planet. They have very specific ideas of what constitutes a desirable citizen: no Quoppina who isn't a Voion seems to qualify—"

"Get to the point!"

"You Rhoon, not being Voion, are going to have to join the fight—"

"A curious fancy, that!" the Rhoon bassooned. "As though the lofty Rhoon-folk would stoop to such petty enterprise!"

"I wonder if that keen vision of yours has detected the presence of a number of Rhoon cruising around at treetop level over the jungle in the last few days?"

"Those did I note, and wondered at it," the Rhoon conceded. "But a Rhoon flies where he will—"

"Does he?" Retief countered. "Those particular Rhoon are flying where the Voion will."

"Nonsense! A Rhoon, servant to a creeping mite who'd not a goodly swallow make?"

"They have at least two squadrons of Rhoon in service now, and unless someone changes their plans for them, there'll be more recruits in the very near future. You, for example—"

"Gerthudion, slave to a verminous crawler on the floor of the world?" The Rhoon spun its wide rotors with an ominous buzzing sound. "Not while I live!"

"Exactly," Retief agreed.

"What mean you?" the Rhoon croaked. "What mad talk is this . . .?"

"Those Rhoon the Voion are using are all dead," Retief said flatly. "The Voion killed them and they're riding around on their corpses."

Gerthudion sat squatted on folded legs, her stilled rotors canted at non-aeronautical angles.

"This talk, it makes no sense," she tubaed. "Dead Rhoon, their innards to replace with wires imported from a factory on another world? Power cells instead of stomachs? Usurping Voion strapped into saddles in place of honest Rhoonish brains?"

"That's about it. You Quoppina all have organo-electronic interiors, and there's enough metal in your makeup to simplify spot welding the necessary replacement components in position. A nuclear pack the size of a fat man's lunch will supply enough power to run even those king-sized rotors of yours for a year. I didn't have time to examine the dead Rhoon I saw in detail, but I'd guess they've even rigged the oculars to a cockpit display screen to take advantage of your natural vision. Riding your zombies, the Voion can probably fly higher and faster than you can—"

"They'd dare?" the Rhoon burst out, vibrating her posterior antennae in the universal Gesture of Propriety Outraged. "Our airy realm to usurp—our very members to employ? Aunt Vulugulei—for a week her dainty tonnage I've not seen; could it be . . .?"

"Quite possibly she's been fitted out with a windshield and rudder pedals," Retief nodded. "And some shined-up

Voion's probably sitting where her main reactor used to be, carving his initials on her side and revving her rotors—"

"Enough! No more!" The Rhoon waggled her oculars in a dizzying pattern. She rose, creaking, on legs quivering with emotion, started her rotors up. "I'm off, my fellow Rhoon to consult," she called over the rising tumult of air. "If what you say is true—and I've a horrid feeling it is—we'll join in, these ghouls to destroy!"

"I had an idea you'd see it that way, Gertie. And don't forget to ask if any of them have seen a party of Stilters in the jungle."

"Inquire I will; meantime, my eggs from that precarious edge withdraw. If one should slip, your ragtag horde will lack a leader!" In a hailstorm of blown pebbles, the Rhoon leaped off, beating her way eastward toward a cluster of tall peaks.

Retief turned at a sound—a loud *scrongg!* like a sheet-metal roof being lifted off a shed by a high wind. The heap of eggs which he had stacked safely back where he had found them quivered. The ripping noise came again; a gleaming spike poked out through the polished curve of the center spheroid in the bottom row, ripped a foot-long tear. An ungainly shape thrust through the opening —a head like a chromalloy pickax equipped with a pair of alert eyes which fixed on Retief. The beak opened.

"Quopp!" the fledgling Rhoon squalled. "Quopppp!" It struggled frantically, snapping the impressive jaws, lined, Retief noted, with a row of triangular razors. A clawed leg appeared, gained the newcomer another six inches of freedom. As the broached egg rocked, those above trembled, then toppled with a crash like a spilled milk cans. One, badly dented, bounced to a stop at Retief's feet. A six-inch split opened to reveal a second baby face, complete with meat shredders. The first Rhoonlet gave a final kick, sprawled free of the shell, which skidded across the platform, driven by the wind, disappeared over the side. A third egg gave a jump; a bright needle point punctured its side.

The first of the newborn Rhoon was unsteadily on its feet now, trying out six short, unspecialized limbs, claw-tipped, the rear pair showing only knobby buds where later the rotating members would develop—a form not unlike the ten-million-year remote ancestor of all the Quopp tribes. The hatchling wobbled, steadied, then charged, jaws gaping. Retief sidestepped, noting that infant number two was now half clear of his prison, while number three was surveying the scene with interested eyes. Dull clunks and clangs attested to activity within the other three eggs.

The eldest infant managed to halt its rush just short of the cliff edge, teetered for a moment staring down into the awesome depths over which it would soar later in life, backed away, hissing, then remembered lunch and rushed Retief again in time to collide with younger brother, freshly on the scene. While the two tangled, squalling, Retief hastily maneuvered half a dozen scattered rocks in place to form a rude barricade, stationed himself behind it. The argument ended as a third young appetite shot past the combatants, zeroing in on the free lunch. The trio hit the barrier with a metallic crash, rebounded, came on again—and now there were four.

The beat of heavy rotors sounded above. Gerthudion, flanked by two immense males distinguished by gold and red cranial plumes, dropped in with a tornado of air that sent her young slithering and squawking across the rocky platform—and over the edge.

"Hey!" Retief called. "Your kids . . ."

The Rhoon settled in. "That's all right; obnoxious creatures, those. It's only the eggs I'm concerned about, their hatching to ensure. Anyway, they'll be all right. It's good experience. As for the call to war, we're with you—"

A small head appeared over the edge; scrabbling claws pulled a hungry Rhoonlet up, the others close behind. Retief stepped to the giant parent, scaled the massive side and straddled the back just behind the head. "Let's get moving," he called over the pound of idling rotors. "I'm beginning to share your view of the younger generation."

"As for your Terries," Gerthudion honked, "Lundelia reports he's seen such a group as you described near the village of the Herpp, a few miles west."

"Then just drop me off there, if you don't mind."

The Rhoon leaped into the air, the backwash from her pounding rotors a howling typhoon.

"I'll take you there," she boomed over the uproar.

"Then thereafter you'll guide me to these ghoulish Voion, my vengeance to wreak."

It was a swift flight from the chill altitudes of the rock spires down across rolling jungle to the bend of the river where the pinkish copperwood huts of the Herpp nestled in the shelter of the trees. Gerthudion settled in to a bouncy landing on a sand spit where there was clearance for her rotors, and Retief slid down, settled his sword belt into position for a quick draw, scanning the silent village with its neat wheelways, orderly flower beds, and colorful awnings.

"Nobody in sight, Gertie; I think the inhabitants beat a hasty retreat when they saw you coming."

"Or mayhap they crouch behind their doorposts with drawn bows," the flyer suggested.

"Yeah—mayhap. I guess there's just one way to find out." He walked across the sand, climbed a grassy bank, stood at the end of the village street beside a long table heaped with bright-colored fruits and fragments of husk— a task apparently hastily abandoned.

"I am Tief-tief," he called. "And I dance the Dance of Friendly Intentions."

There was a flicker of motion at a window. The polished tip of an arrow poked into view, followed by a pale blue head.

"I am Nop-Nee, and I dance the Dance of Fair Warning," a squeaky-chalk voice piped.

"I'm looking for some friends of mine," Retief called. "Don't let Gerthudion bother you. She's tame—"

The Rhoon snorted loudly behind Retief.

". . . and she won't eliminate your village unless you carelessly initiate hostilities by letting fly with that arrow."

The aimed weapon disappeared. The Herpp rose, emerged cautiously from the door, the arrow still nocked but aimed off-side now.

"What makes you think your friends are here?" he chirped.

"Oh, word gets around. There are ten of them— Stilters, you know. Where are they?"

"Never saw them," the Herpp snapped. "Now you better get back on that monster of yours and dust back off where you came from, before we clobber the both of you."

"Don't do anything hasty, Nop-Nee," Retief cautioned. "Gerthudion is a patient Rhoon, but you *might* annoy her with that kind of talk—"

"Bah, we've seen enough Rhoon in the last twelve hours to last us," the Herpp snapped. "A round dozen of the devils flew over and dropped stones on us last night; told us to surrender, before they set the whole place on fire!"

"That's unfortunate," Retief agreed. "But those were outlaw Rhoon. Gerthudion's on her way to hunt them down right now—"

"Then she'd better get started. We've got catapults and ballistae rigged, and by now they're zeroed in and ready to fire. So . . ." he raised the bow. "Scat!"

"I admire your spirit," Retief said. "But first I want the ten Terrans."

Nop-Nee drew the bowstring farther back. "Not on your life! I'm not turning harmless foreigners over to the likes of you and your oversized cronies! They're guests of Quopp, and they'll receive hospitable treatment. I am Nop-Nee and I dance the Dance of Ferocious Defiance!"

"And I'm Retief and I dance the Dance of Mounting Impatience—"

"You can dance the Dance of Apoplexy for all I care," Nop-Nee yelped. "Git!"

"Retief cupped a hand beside his mouth.

"Girls, if you're in there, come on out!" He called in Teran. "I'm here on behalf of the Terry Embassy at Ixix . . ."

The The Herpp jumped back in alarm. "Here, I'm Nop-Nee and I dance the Dance of Confusion! That sounded like Tery talk . . ."

A door banged wide on the third hut in line, and a slim brunette Terry female in torn flying togs appeared. She shaded her eyes at Retief, while other girls crowded out behind her. Retief executed a sweeping bow.

"Ladies, I'm enchanted to find you," he said. "I hope none of you were hurt in the crash."

"Who are you?" the brunette asked. She had a snub nose and blue eyes and was not over nineteen. "I thought I heard a Terran voice . . ."

"That was me, I'm afraid. I'm known as Tief-tief. I'm here to help you."

Nop-Nee was jittering restlessly, keeping the drawn bow aimed at Retief's chest.

"You're not from that nasty little Voion who locked us up in a corral?" the girl asked.

"By no means. He and I are confirmed antagonists, ever since I blew up his liquor vault."

The girls were in a huddle now, whispering together. A small blonde with green eyes spoke urgently, with emphatic gestures.

"Well," the brunette said. "I guess we may as well take a chance; Aphrodisia likes your voice." She smiled and came forward. "I'm Rene. It's very nice of you to trouble about us, Mr. Tief-tief."

Nop-Nee lowered his bow. "I dance the Dance of Utter Bafflement," he complained. "What's going on?"

"Girls, now that I've located you, I can make arrangements to fly you out. I'm afraid Ixix isn't a healthy place for Terries right now, but there's a trading post at Rum Jungle where you'll be reasonably safe for the present." Retief looked over the little group, all young, all pretty, all showing signs of a difficult day and night in the jungle.

"Which one of you is Fifi?" he inquired.

The girls looked at each other. Rene bit her lip. "She's not here, I'm afraid. We heard that a rebel army was organizing to fight the Voion, and she started out early this morning alone to try to reach them."

"You ladies just sit tight until you hear from me," Retief called down from his perch on Gerthudion's back. "I'll round up a few Rhoon and be back for you as soon as I can."

"I am Nop-Nee and I dance the Dance of Apology," the Herpp keened. "Who would have thought that a Stilter on Rhoonback would mean anything but trouble?"

"You did just the right thing, Nop-Nee," Retief assured the agitated Herpp. "Take good care of the girls until I get back, and we'll all dance the Dance of Mutual Congratulation."

"She wouldn't *let* any of us go with her," Aphrodisia wailed. "She said we'd slow her down . . ."

"Don't worry. We should be able to spot her from the

air." Retief waved; Gerthudion lifted off with a great battering of air, climbed to three hundred feet, headed south. It was high noon now; the sun glared down from a cloudless pale sky. Retief watched the trail below, saw the scurry of small Quoppina fleeing the shadow of the giant flyer passing overhead—but no sign of the missing girl.

It was a twenty-minute flight to the spot where the victorious troops of the Federated Tribes had been encamped eight hours earlier. Gerthudion settled in to a landing on the wheel-trampled ground, deserted now and littered with the debris of battle—and of hasty evacuation.

"Looks like our prisoners sneaked off when nobody was looking," Retief observed. He studied the maze of trails leading off in all directions. "Which way did our lads go?" he inquired of a pair of Phips, hovering nearby.

"Here-here, there-there," the nearest cheeped. "Run-run, quick-quick!"

"Don't tell me," Retief said. "Some of our more impulsive members started in on the chore of sawing the Voion up into convenient lenghts, thereby panicking them into breaking out of the jam."

"Check-check!" a Phip agreed. "All-all scat-scat!"

"And by now they're scattered over a hundred square miles of jungle, with several thousand highly irritated Voion in pursuit. So much for the grass-roots movement—"

"Tief-tief!" a Phip buzzed in excitedly from a reconnoiter of the nearby cover. "Thing-thing, there-there!"

Retief drew his sword. "What kind of thing, small stuff? A Voion left over from the party?"

"Big-big, long-long, stilt-stilt!"

"A Stilter? Like me? Gertie, wait here!" Retief followed the Phip for a hundred yards, then paused, listening.

There was a crackling in the underbrush. A heavy-shouldered biped stalked into view—an unshaven Terran in a tattered coverall and scuffed boots, holding a heavy old-style power pistol gripped in one immense fist.

"Hold it right there, Bug," Big Leon growled in tribal dialect. "I got a couple bones to pick with you."

Retief smiled behind the mask, put a hand up to lift the disguising headpiece—

"Keep the flippers out from the sides," Leon growled in dialect. "And drop the sticker. Maybe you never saw one of these before—" he gestured with the gun "—but it'll blow a hole through you, tree and all."

Retief tossed the sword aside. Leon nodded. "Smart Bug. Now, there's just one thing I want out of you, wiggly-eyes: I hear there's a native leader that's popped up out here in the brush, organizing the yokels." He motioned at the spare-parts littered ground. "It looks like there was a little action here, not too many hours back. I don't know which side you were on, and I don't care —just tell me where to find that Bug leader—fast."

"Why?" Retief demanded.

Leon frowned at him. "For a Bug, you've got kind of a funny voice—but to hell with it. I want to ask him for help."

"What kind of help?"

Leon drew a finger across his forehead like a windshield wiper, slung sweat from it. "Help in staying alive," he said. "There's forty-six of us Terries over at Rum Jungle. Ikk's got us surrounded with about half a million troops and he swears he's going to eat us for breakfast."

"I see," Retief nodded. "And you'd ask a Bug for help?"

"We'll take any help we can get," Leon stated flatly.

"What makes you think you can get it?"

Leon grunted. "You got a point there—but let's can the chatter. Where'll I find this Tief-tief character?"

Retief folded his arms. "That's what they call me," he said.

"Huh?" Leon's mouth closed slowly. "Uh-huh," he nodded. "It figures. The only Quopp on the planet I want to make pals with, and I stick a gun in his chest-plates." He holstered the weapon. "Well, how about it?"

"I'd like to help you—" Retief said.

"Great. That's settled, then. Call your army out of the bushes and let's get rolling. Something tells me the Voion will hit us at dawn—"

"As I was saying," Retief interrupted, "I'd like to help you Terries, but unfortunately I seem to have misplaced my army."

Leon's hand went to his gun. "What kind of a stall is this?" he grated.

"My hundred seasoned veterans wandered off while I wasn't looking," Retief explained.

"A hundred!" The big Terran burst out. "I heard you had half the Bugs on Quopp with you! I heard you were cutting Ikk's troops into Christmas tree ornaments! I heard—"

"You heard wrong. The Federated Tribes were a spark glimmering in the night. Now they're not even that."

Big Leon let out a long breath. "So I had a little walk for nothing. OK. I should have known better. Now all I've got to do is get back through the Voion lines so I can help the boys pick off as many of those Jaspers as we can before they ride over us." He half turned away, then faced Retief again. "A hundred against an army, huh? Maybe you Bugs are all right—some of you." He turned and was gone.

Retief motioned a hovering Phip over.

"No sign of any other Stilters in the neighborhood?"

"Not-not," the Phip stated.

"How each one of you fellows knows what all the other ones know beats me," Retief said. "But that's a mystery I'll have to investigate later. Keep looking for her; she can't have gotten far through this growth in the dark with a Voion behind every third clump of brush."

"Sure-sure, Tief-tief! Look-look!" the Phip squeaked and darted off. Retief pulled off his helmet, unbuckled the chest and back armor, laid it aside with a sigh of relief. He removed the leg coverings gingerly; there was a nasty blister above the ankle where the Voion jailer had plied his torch carelessly. Clad in the narrow-cut trousers and shirt he had retained when donning his disguise in Sopp's shop, he stacked the armor together, tied it with a loop of wire vine, concealed it behind a bush, then made his way back to the place where he had left Gerthudion.

"All right, let's go, Gertie," he called, coming up her port quarter. The Rhoon started nervously, tilted a foot-long ocular over her dorsal plates, then gave a rumbling growl.

"It's all right," Retief soothed. "I'm wearing a disguise."

"You look like a Terry," Gerthudion accused.

"That's right; it's all part of an elaborate scheme I'm rapidly getting wrapped up in like King Tut."

"Kink Tut? Who's he? Sounds like a Voion. Now royal they'll declare themselves—?"

"Steady, girl. Just a literary allusion."

"But now, Tief-tief, what of dear Aunt Vulugulei, I long to seek her out, or her destoyers to rend!"

"I'm afraid you Rhoon are on your own, Gertie. Those fighting tribes I told you about won't be available to carry out their end of the war after all."

"No matter; even now the tribal host circles far to the west in a wide sweep, our enemies to spy. Then retribution will me take in full measure—allies or no."

"How long would it take them to get here?"

"Many hours, Tief-tief—if their search they'd abandon to heed a call."

"Do you know where Rum Jungle is?"

"Certainly—if by that you mean that clustering of huts yonder to the south, whence emanate curious odors of alien cookery with a disfavorable wind—"

"That's the place. I need a lift in there. And there's another Stilter up ahead; he's wearing the same kind of disguise I am. We can gather him in on the way."

"As you wish, Tief-tief."

"Gertie, now that the Federated Tribes are dispersed, I can't hold you to our agreement. This is a dangerous trip I'm asking you to make. You might run into the whole Voion Air Force."

"Why then, I'll know where to find the ghouls!" Gerthudion honked. "Mount up, Retief! Fly where I will, that will I—and let the villains beware!"

"That's the way to talk, Gertie."

Retief climbed into position on the Rhoon's back. "Now let's go see if things at Rum Jungle are as bad as reported—or worse."

9

"I don't get it," Big Leon said between clenched teeth from his position just behind Retief atop Gerthudion's ribbed shoulder-plates. "How'd you get out here in the woods? How'd you spot me? And how in the name of the Big Worm did you tame this man-eater? In forty years in the jungle I never—"

"You never tried," Retief finished for him.

"I guess I didn't," Leon sounded surprised. "Why would I?"

"We're sitting on one reason. I'll go into the other answers later, when things quiet down."

Gerthudion's rotors thumped rhythmically; wind whistled past Retief's head. A thousand feet below, the jungle was a gray-green blanket, touched with yellow light here and there where the afternoon sun reached a tall treetop.

"Hey, Retief!" Leon called above the whine of the slipstream. "Has your friend here got a friend?"

Retief looked back, following Big Leon's pointing arm. Half a mile behind, a Rhoon was rapidly overhauling the laden Gerthudion.

"Goblin at seven o'clock," Retief called to her. "Anyone you know, Gertie?"

The Rhoon lifted her massive head, then swung her body sideways—a trick she performed with only a slight lagging of forward motion.

"That's—but it couldn't be Not Aunt Vulugulei" the great creature honked. At once, she banked, swept in a tight curve back toward the trailing Rhoon, now closing fast.

"Aunt Vulgy!" she trumpeted. "Where in Quopp have you been? I've been worrying myself into a premature molt—"

The other Rhoon, a scant five hundred yards distant now, banked up suddenly, shot away, rising fast, its rotors whick-whicking loudly. Gerthudion swerved, causing her riders to grab for better holds, gave chase.

"Auntie! It's me, Gerthudion! Wait . . . !" The agitated flyer was beating her rotors frantically as she fell behind the unladen Rhoon, a quarter of a mile ahead now and two hundred feet higher. Sunlight glinted on spinning rotors as the strange Rhoon tilted, swung in a tight curve, swept down at top speed on its pursuer.

"Duck!" Retief called. "It's a zombie!"

Yellow light winked from a point behind the pouncing Rhoon's head. The buzz of a power gun cut through the tumult of rushing air. There was a harsh rattle of sound from behind Retief; blue light glared and danced at close hand as a pencil-thin beam lanced out, picked out the attacking Rhoon's left rotor, held on it as Gerthudion wheeled to the left, dropped like a stone, rocking violently in the air blast as the enemy flyer shot past.

"I nicked him," Leon growled. "The range is too long for a handgun to do much damage."

"He's got the same problem." Retief leaned forward. "Gertie, I'm sorry about Aunt Vulugulei, but you see how it is. Try to get above him; he can't fire through his rotors."

"I'll try, Tief-tief," Gerthudion wailed. "To think that my own auntie—"

"It's not your aunt anymore, Gertie; just a sneaky little Voion getting a free ride."

Gerthudion's rotors labored. "I can't gain on her—or it," she bawled. "Not with this burden . . ."

"Tell her not to try dumping us off," Leon barked. "My gun is the only thing that'll nail that Jasper! Just get me in position!"

The Voion-controlled Rhoon cadaver was far above now, still climbing. Gerthudion, her rotors thumping hard, was losing ground.

"He'll drop on us again in a minute," Retief said. "Gertie, as he gets within range, you're going to have to go into a vertical bank to give Leon a clear shot . . ."

"Vertical? I'll fall like a stone from a frost-shattered peak!"

"That's the way it's got to be, I'm afraid. Lead him down—and don't flare out until we're at treetop level. If we give him time to think, it will dawn on him all he has to do is stay right over us and pour in the fire!"

"I'll try . . ." The Rhoon was in position now, above and slightly off-side to the right. It stooped then, moving in for an easy kill. Gerthudion held her course; abruptly the enemy gun fired, a wide-angle beam at extreme range that flicked across Retief's exposed face like a breath from a blast furnace.

"Now," Retief called. Instantly, Gerthudion whipped up on her left side, her rotors screaming in the sudden release of load, and in the same moment Leon, his left arm clamped around Retief, lanced out with his narrow-beam weapon. A spot of actinic light darted across the gray belly-plates of the zombie, then found and held steady on the left rotor.

The fire from above was back on target now, playing over Gerthudion's exposed side-plates with an odor like hot iron.

"Stay with that wide beam another ten seconds, and you're a gone Bug," Leon grated out. The Rhoon above dipped to one side now, feeling the sting of the blaster, but Leon followed, held the rotor in the beam while air shrieked up past him like a tornado.

"Right myself now I must, or perish!" Gerthudion honked. "Which is it to be, Tief-tief?"

"Pull out!" Retief grabbed for handholds as the great body shifted under him, surging upward with crushing pressure. The whirling vanes bit into air, hammering; Leon broke off his fire—

"Hey, look!" The attacking Rhoon had veered off at the last possible instant, gun still firing; now lazily it rolled over, went into a violent tumble. Pieces flew; then the zombie was gone against the darkness below.

"I think you burned through his wiring," Retief called. "Gertie, stay low now; it's only another couple of miles."

"Low shall I stay, like it or no," the Rhoon called. "I thought my main armature, its windings I would melt!"

Retief felt the heat of the overworked body scorching his legs. "If we meet another one in the air we've had it."

"If far it is, we're lost," she wheezed. "I'm all but spent . . ."

"There it is!" Leon pointed to a tiny cluster of buildings against the sweep of jungle ahead, ringed by tilled fields.

Gerthudion flew on, dropping even lower, until she labored just above the high crowns of trees whose leaves glittered in her backwash like rippling water. The forest ended abruptly, and she was swooping across the fields that surrounded the trading town, packed solid now with Voion soldiery.

"Look at 'em," Leon called. "Jammed in so tight they can't even maneuver! If those Bugs knew anything about siege tactics, they'd have wiped us out the first night!"

"Better try some evasive action," Retief called. "They may have some big stuff down there."

Gerthudion groaned, complied sluggishly.

"If they have, they're holding it back," Leon yelled behind him. "All they hit us with so far is a lot of talk, plenty of rocks and arrows, and a few handguns."

Blasters winked below now, searching after the Rhoon as she threw her massive weight from one side to another, flying a twisting course toward the squatty palisade ahead and the cluster of low buildings behind it. Leon took careful aim, poured a long burst from his power gun into a Voion gun crew. There was a flicker, then a violent burst of pale yellow light that puffed outward in a dingy smoke cloud, faded quickly as fragments whistled past Gerthudion's head and clattered against her rotors. Then the giant flyer staggered over the wall in a billow of dust, slammed the ground at the center of the wide central plaza of the town. Men appeared, running toward the Rhoon.

"Hold your fire!" Big Leon bellowed. "It's me—and Retief! This Rhoon's a tame one! The first bushwhacker lays a hand on her's got me to answer to!"

The embattled Terrans were all around now, gaping as Retief and Leon slid down from their places.

"Jumping jinkberries, Leon—how'd you catch that critter?"

"You sure it don't bite?"

". . . thought you was one of them that been buzzing us all day—"

"—how about it, Leon? Did you find that Bug chief?"

"Quiet, the lot of you!" Leon held up his hands. "The bug rebels are out of the picture. We're on our own." He motioned to Retief. "I picked up a recruit, name's Retief."

"Well, you're just in time for the massacre, Mister," someone greeted.

"Hey, Leon—what about this Rhoon of yours? Maybe it could airlift us out of here—"

"I'll carry no burden . . . this day," the Rhoon gasped out. Her rotors sagged as she squatted, her massive keel against the ground. "Grave damage . . . to my windings . . . I fear I've done . . . such burdens to bear up . . . the while I gamboled like a Phip . . ."

"You did OK, Gertie," Leon said. "Just take it easy, girl." He faced the crowd of some forty unshaven, unwashed frontiersmen. "What's been going on while I was gone?"

"They hit us again just after First Eclipse," a wide, swarthy man with a low-slung pistol belt said. "Same old business: Come at us in a straight frontal assault, whooping it up and shooting arrows; a couple Rhoon making passes, dropping leaflets and stones; our guns—we still got three working—kept 'em at a safe altitude. We kept our heads down and peppered 'em and they pulled back before they hit the stockade. They been quiet since noon—but they're up to something. Been working since before dawn on something."

Leon grunted. "After a while those Bugs are going to figure out all they have to do is hit us from four sides at once, get a couple magnesium fires going against the walls, and we've had it."

"Their tactics are likely to improve suddenly," Retief said. "There's a Groaci military adviser in the area. I imagine he'll take the troops in hand before many hours pass. In the meantime, we'd better start making some plans—"

"Some wills, you mean," someone corrected. "They'll flatten us like a tidal wave once they get rolling."

"Still, we don't want to make it too easy for them. Leon, what have you got in the way of armaments, other than those three guns I heard mentioned?"

"My iron makes four; it's got about half a charge left. There's a couple dozen heavy-duty hunting bows; some of the boys are pretty good with 'em—and I had Jerry trying to tinker up a rig to drop a few thousand volts to the perimeter wall—"

"I have it going, Leon," Jerry called. "Don't know how long it will last if they throw a big load on the line."

"We finished up the ditching while you was gone, Leon," a man called. "If they get past the stockade, they'll hit a six-foot trench; that ought to slow 'em down some."

"This is all just peanuts," Leon said. "Sure, we'll take a few hundred with us—but that won't stop us from going."

"It will be dusk in another few hours," Retief said. "I think we can count on a go-for-broke attack before then, with General Hish calling the plays. Let's see if we can't arrange a suitable reception."

From a top-floor room in a tower that formed one corner of the compound at Rum Jungle Retief studied the ranks of the Voion that moved restlessly all across the half-mile of cleared ground surrounding the fortress.

"Uh-huh, our Groaci military expert is on the scene," he said. "That formation's not exactly a parade-ground effect, but it's a long way from the mob we flew over on the way in."

"It's not that that gives me the willies," a thick-set man with a short blond beard said. "It's them damned Rhoon circling up there." He motioned toward floating dots far overhead that indicated the presence of a pair of the huge flyers.

"If they knew Gertie's crowd were out looking for them, they'd be a little less carefree up there," Retief commented. "But I'm afraid our aerial allies are combing the wrong stretch of sky."

A man hurried in, breathing hard. "OK, Big Leon," he said. "I guess that does it: We rigged the ropes and the tank-traps, and all the boys are posted up as high as they could get. Les's got a good head o' steam up on both boilers, and—"

"All right, Shorty," Leon said. "Just tell everybody to look sharp and don't make a move before the signal goes up."

"Get ready," Retief said. "I think something's starting down there now."

Barely visible in the dim light, the Voion were crowding back, opening narrow lanes through their ranks; bulky shapes were trundling forward along the paths thus formed.

"Oh-oh, looks like they got some kind of heavy equipment," Shorty said.

"Nope—not equipment; friends," Leon stated. "Those are Jackoo. I guess that cuts it. Those boys can steamroller right through the walls."

"Correction," Retief said. "Six, two, and even those are zombies—like the Rhoon."

"What do you mean?" Leon and the other stared at Retief. He gave them a brief explanation of the Voion technique of installing an energy cell and a pilot in a dead Quoppina.

"The drive mechanism and circuitry are all there," he concluded. "All they have to do is supply the power and the guidance."

"That's far from simple," Jerry said. "Ye gods, the technical knowledge that implies . . . ! Maybe we've been underestimating these Voion!"

"I think the Groaci have a digit in the pie," Retief said.

"Groaci, huh," Jerry nodded, looking worried. "It fits; they're skillful surgeons as well as exporters of sophisticated electronic and mechanical devices—"

"How can they butt in here?" Shorty demanded. "I thought that kind of stuff was frowned on by the CDT."

"You have to get within frowning range first," Retief pointed out. "They've done a good job of keeping under cover."

"Looks like they're getting set to hit the wall, all right," Leon said. "I count eight of 'em. The game'll be over quicker'n I figured."

Retief studied the maneuvers below, dim in the predawn light. "Maybe not," he said. "See if you can get me seven volunteers, and we'll try to stretch it into extra innings."

Retief waited, flattened against the wall of a one-story structure the back of which was no more than ten feet from the timber wall surrounding the compound.

"Get ready," Shorty called from the roof above. "They're rolling now; boy, look at 'em come! Brace yourself—he's gonna hit right—"

There was a thunderous smash; a section of wall six feet wide bowed, burst inward; amid a hail of splinters, the dull magenta form of a two-ton Jackoo appeared, wobbling from the terrific force of the impact, but still coming on, veering past the corner of the structure half in its path, gathering speed again now as it plunged past Retief at a distance of six feet—

He swung out behind the bulky shape, took three running steps, jumped, pulled himself up on the wide back—even broader than Fufu's ponderous dimensions, he noted in passing. Directly before him, in a hollow chopped out behind the massive skull—the brain location in all Quoppina species—the narrow back of a Voion crouched, a heavy helmet of gray armor plate protecting the head. Retief braced himself, reached forward, hauled the driver bodily from his cockpit, propelled him over the prow; there was a heavy ker-blump! as the broad wheels slammed over the unfortunate Quoppina. Clinging to the now unguided zombie, Retief reached into the cockpit, flipped up a large lever dabbed with luminescent orange paint. The groan of the drive ceased instantly; the juggernaut slowed, rolled to a stop a foot from the six-foot moat dug by the defenders.

There was a confused shrilling behind; Retief turned, saw the leaders of a column of Voion pressing through the broached wall.

"Now!" someone shouted from a rooftop. At once, a brilliant cascade of electric blue sparks leaped across the packed mass of invaders struggling on high wheels across the shattered timbers; the two foremost members squalled, shot forward; those behind also squalled, but impeded by the uneven ground and the efforts of their fellows, failed to dart clear. The high voltage continued to flow—here leaping a gap to the accompaniment of miniature lightnings, there bringing adjacent patches of Voion to red heat before welding them together. More Voion, coming up fast from the rear, joined the press, found themselves instantly joined in the wild dance of arcing current and randomly stimulated nerves and gear trains.

Retief returned to the task at hand, flipped the "back" switch, hastily maneuvered the captured ram to face in the direction from which it had come. The two Voion who had leaped clear of the confusion dashed toward him, seeking refuge. Retief grabbed up the issue club dropped by the former operator in his hasty exit in time to slam the gun from the grip of one of them, knock the other spinning with a backhanded swipe to the head. Then he pushed the "go" lever into the forward position, threw the speed control full over, and vaulted over the side.

"Cut the power," Shorty yelled from above. At once, the showering sparks from the electrified attack column died, leaving only the dull red glow of hot spots; then the riderless zombie was into the welded mass, slamming through the obstruction to disappear into the mob beyond.

"Get them cables back in place!" a voice yelled. Men darted out, hauled at the one-inch steel lines, stretching them across the gap three feet from ground level. Retief looked around. Across the compound, other dark gaps showed in the wall. Here and there lay the slumped form of a Voion, and one Jackoo bulked, immobile.

"Six of 'em busted through," Big Leon's voice said, coming up beside Retief, breathing hard. "One got stuck in his own hole; another one was damaged—couldn't get him going again. The boys sent the others back to spread joy according to plan."

"Any casualties?"

"Les got a busted arm; he was kind of slow knocking over a Bug that got through. Your scheme worked out neat, Retief."

"It slowed them a little. Let's see how Gertie's doing."

They walked across to where the big flyer still rested, her four legs sprawled, her eyes dull.

"Gertie, they'll make it through on the next try," Retief said. "How are you feeling?"

"Bad," the Rhoon groaned. "My circuitry I've overloaded. A month's nest-rest I'll require to be myself again."

"You're going to have to lift off in a few minutes or you'll wind up being somebody else," Big Leon said. "Think you can do it?"

Gerthudion lifted an eye, gazed distastefully across at

the signs of the recent fray. "If I must, I must. But I'll wait until the last, my powers to recover."

"Gertie, I have an important mission for you," Retief said.

He outlined the plan while Gerthudion breathed sonorously, like a pipe organ being tuned.

". . . that's about it," he concluded. "Can you do it?"

" 'Tis no mean errand you dispatch me on, Retief; still, I'll aloft, these dastards to forestall. Then I'll return, your further needs to serve."

"Thanks, Gertie. I'm sorry I got you into this."

"I came willingly," she honked with a show of spirit. "Sorry am I my fellow Rhoon so far afield have flown, else a goodly number of the rascals we'd have disassembled for you." She started her rotors with a groan, lifted off, a vast dark shadow flitting upward in the gloom, tilting away toward the dark wall of the jungle.

10

"Hey," Shorty shouted from his rooftop. "There's a bunch shaping up to hit the gap over here—and looks like the same down the line at Jerry's spot . . ."

Other calls rang out from the spotters posted on the roofs.

"Trying to catch us off-balance," Big Leon said. "OK," he yelled up to Shorty. "You know the plan; don't let yourselves get cut off!" He turned to Retief as they started for the buildings at a run. "That Groaci general's spending Bugs like half-credit chips in an all-night Zoop Palace."

"He's getting them free," Retief said. "So far they haven't bought him much."

"Here they come . . ." Shorty's voice was drowned in a shrill battle cry as the lead elements of the new wave of Voion shot through the breaks in the stockade, coming fast along the paths trodden out by the Jackoo. The first in line—a big fellow with gaudy tribal inlays—saw Retief and Leon, veered toward them raising a barb-headed spear, struck the stretched cable and slammed to a stop, bent almost double—and was instantly engulfed by others charging in to collide from behind with a sound like empty garbage cans falling off a truck.

"Sock it to 'em!" Les yelled from his vantage point in the corner tower. Again a display of fireworks sprang up as ten thousand volts surged through the strung cable.

"The generators can't take that load for long," Big Leon yelled above the uproar of crackling current, screeching Voion, and enthusiastic human yells.

There was a brief tremor underfoot, a vivid glare from the direction of the power plant. Retief and Leon threw themselves flat as a dull boom rumbled across the compound accented by the whine of shrapnel passing overhead. The glow at the fence line died.

"Shorty!" Leon called.

"He's down," a voice rang from the next post in line.

Leon swore, jumped to his feet. "Fall back on the post office," he yelled. "Pass the word!" He turned, ran for the building where Shorty had been posted. The Voion crowded in the gap in the wall were shrilling, fighting to free themselves—those who had survived the overload. A large specimen broke free, shot forward to cut Leon off. Retief reached him in time to lay a solid blow across the side of his head, then spiked his wheels with his own club. Ahead, Leon jumped, caught the eaves, pulled himself up. A second Voion disentangled himself, came thumping forward on a warped wheel, gun in hand—

There was the crackle of a power gun from the upper window of the adjacent corner tower. The Voion's head disappeared in a spatter of vaporized metallo-chitin as the dead chassis slammed on to crash against the wall. Leon reappeared, lowering the inert form of Shorty. Retief caught the wounded man, draped him over a shoulder as Leon dropped down beside him.

"Let's sprint," the big man said. "They'll cut us off . . . !"

Half a dozen Voion wheeled around the corner of the next structure in line, charged the two Terrans. Retief pivoted aside from a blaster shot, clubbed the next Voion in line as shots burped from the tower. At his side, Leon ducked under a swinging club, caught a Voion by the wheel, flipped him. Then they were through, sprinting for the plank laid across the six foot ditch. Leon spun, flipped the board into the trench. Shots scored the doorframe as they dived through it.

"Close," Leon panted. "How's Shorty?"

"Breathing." Retief took the stairs three at a time, whirled into the room previously selected as a last-ditch stronghold, lowered the small man to the floor, then jumped to the window. Below, Voion were pouring into the compound—and stopping short at the moat barring their path, in which some dozens of their more impetuous comrades were already trapped, floundering on broken wheels and waving frantic arms. More Voion pressed from behind, crowding those in front. The rank lining the ditch was fighting now to pull back from the brink of disaster but as Retief watched, one, then three more, then half a dozen together went over, dropped with a smash as those behind pressed forward to share in the loot.

"That's one way to bridge it," a man said beside Retief. More men were coming into the room behind him. Across the compound, Retief saw two men drop from a roof, start across, change course as Voion blaster shots crackled near them. A power gun buzzed beside Retief, laying down a covering fire.

"Everybody's here but Sam and Square-deal Mac," somebody yelled.

"They're OK—so far," the man beside Retief called. He fired again, nailed a Voion who had struggled across the Voion-filled moat. One of the two men stumbled, spun, fell on his back. The other bent, slung him over his shoulders in a fireman's carry, came on, disappeared into the door below.

"All in," somebody called. "Button her up!"

There was a sound of heavy timbers falling as a previously prepared barricade dropped into position blocking the door below.

"Henry's had it," somebody said. "Steel splinter in the skull . . ."

"How many we lose?" Leon demanded.

"Henry's dead. Shorty don't look good. Three more with medium bad blaster burns and a couple bruised up."

"Pretty good," somebody called. "We must of put a couple hundred of them devils out of commission just on that last go-round!"

"Their turn comes next," Les said from the window. "They're across the ditch now . . ."

The compound was rapidly filling with Voion, pouring

through the shattered wall and across the choked ditch. The late afternoon light was failing rapidly now.

"They'll fire the building next," Retief said. "Leon, let's get the best shooters at the windows and try to discourage them from getting in close."

Leon snapped orders. Men moved to firing positions, readying bows and power guns.

"We're down to three guns," Leon said, "and not enough arrows to make a fellow start any long books."

"We'll make 'em count," someone said. A bowstring twanged, then another. A blaster buzzed. Below, a group of Voion who had reached the embattled post office withdrew hastily, leaving three former comrades lying on their sides, wheels spinning lazily. The enemy horde filled the compound now, formed up in a dense-packed ring around the Terran-occupied tower.

"The boys in the front rank are a little reluctant to grab the glory," Retief commented.

"But the boys behind won't let 'em stop," Big Leon growled. "It's like fighting high tide."

The circle closed; arrows sped, slammed through armor with solid *clunks!* or glanced off a helmet or shoulder-plate to fly high in the air.

"Save the guns for the ones out front," Leon called. "Watch for fire-makers."

Beside Retief, a man made a choked sound, fell backward, an arrow quivering high in his chest. Retief caught up his bow, nocked a bolt, took aim, picked off a Voion wheeling in fast firing a blaster. The gunner veered, crashed over on his side.

"This is fun," somebody called. "But it won't buy us much. Look at them babies come!"

"Hey, they shot some kind of fire-arrow over here," a man yelled from across the wide room. "It's stuck in the wall, burning like a fused tube-lining!"

There were bright flares among the Voion ranks now, then streaks that arced up across the glowing sky, trailing white-hot embers. Most fell short, one or two among the front ranks of the attackers, but there were two solid thuds against the roof overhead. Acrid, chemical-smelling smoke was coiling in the windows from the first hit.

"How about it, men: Do we stay in here and roast, or go out and take a few of 'em with us?" Leon called.

"Let's go get those Jaspers," someone called. There was a shout of agreement. Men were coughing now; there were more thumps against walls and roof. A flaming arrow shot through a glassless window, elicited yells as it slammed the wall opposite, scattering burning globlets of magnesium. A man plucked it out, set it against his bowstring, let fly; there were yells as it sank home against the chest of a big Voion almost directly below. Someone had the door open now; smoke and sparks billowed in. Big Leon cupped his hands to his mouth to shout above the roar of fire and battle:

"You boys at the windows stick till the rest of us are out; keep pouring it to 'em!" He turned, plunged out through smoke.

Retief waited with his bow drawn, the feathers just under his chin. Big Leon appeared below, behind the tumbled logs of the barricade; a Voion charged to meet him, intercepted Retief's arrow instead. Below Retief's window the Voion were pressing close again, driven by the inexorable pressure of those behind. There were three fires burning briskly along Retief's side of the wall now. He loosed an arrow, saw more Voion crowd in; one, hustled by his fellows, fought helplessly, fell into a flame-spouting puddle of melted wood, flared up in a bright green blaze, only to be smothered by others crushing in against him. From behind the barricade, Leon and the other Terrans fired steadily, building up a heap of casualties. Leon vaulted the barrier, climbed up on the stacked Voion, firing down into the press. Retief picked off a Voion with a gun, set another arrow, loosed it, another . . .

"That's it," a man called. "Out of ammo; I'm going down and see if I can't get me a couple barehanded." He disappeared into the smoke, coughing.

At the barricade, Leon was still firing, an arrow entangled in the sleeve of his leather jacket. Retief saw him throw the gun aside, jump down into the small clear space before the tangle of downed Voion, laying about him with a Voion club.

"I guess it's all over," the last of Retief's fellow archers declared. "No more arrows. Reckon I'll go down and meet 'em in the open. Don't much like the idea of frying up here—"

"Hold it," Retief said. "Look there . . ."

Beyond the palisade, a disturbance had broken out on the Voion left flank. A horde of varicolored Quoppina had appeared from the jungle on that quarter, and were rapidly cutting their way through toward the palisade, led by a wedge of Jackoo, one of which, larger than its fellows, a varicolored Quoppina bestrode. Close behind, a fast-moving column of blue-green fighters followed, their fighting claws snapping left and right; behind them, a detachment of yellow-orange warriors swinging bright-edged scythes mowed a path through the Voion ranks. Small purple shadows appeared among the trees, casting ropes which plucked targets from the fleeing Voion rabble to dangle, arms windmilling, above their fellows.

"Hey! That must be that rebel army," the bowman yelled. "Look at 'em come!"

Down below, the clear space before Big Leon was wider now; all across the compound breaks in the Voion ranks were opening. At the walls, Voion backs were visible as the confused attackers crowded out through the ragged gaps broached by the Jackoo zombies to confront the new threat, before which their fellows were streaming away in disorder.

. The Jackoo vanguard dozed onward, cutting a swathe toward the embattled stockade; the varicolored Quoppina rider whirled a flashing blade above a bright red Voion-like head. A small organized group of Voion barred their path, led by a small officer with wobbly wheels; they stood their ground for half a minute, then broke and fled. Below, Leon's men were across the barricade now, firing at retreating backs, jumping huddled dead and wounded to get clear shots at the confused enemy.

"It's a blooming miracle!" a man shouted.

"That must be them guerrilla fighters we heard about!" someone called. "Yippee!"

Retief left the window, went down through the churning smoke, emerged in the front entry hall where two Terrans lay on their backs behind the barricade of logs. He climbed the latter, clambered across fallen Voion, jumped down to stand beside Leon, bleeding from a cut across the cheek.

"I guess that Bug leader just didn't like my looks," the big man said. "Look yonder . . ."

The bright-colored Quoppina who had led the charge

jumped down from the Jackoo, stepped through the nearest gap in the wall—a tall creature with posterior arms well developed for walking, shorter upper members, rudimentary rotors above each shoulder, a bright red-orange face resembling a Voion with the exception of the color.

"Yep," Leon said. "That's Tief-tief, all right. Come on; I guess we owe that Bug some thanks . . ."

Retief studied the varicolored Stilter as it strode across the battle-littered ground, sword in hand, casually skirting the smoking bodies of electrocuted Voion, detouring around victims shot, incinerated, or crushed in the disorderly scene just concluded.

"That was good timing," Big Leon called in the Voion tribal dialect. "Glad you changed your mind."

The Stilter came up, halted facing Retief and Leon, sheathed the sword. "My grasp of the Voion tongue is rather limited," the Quoppina said in clear, accentless Terran, looking around at the shambles. "It seems you gentlemen have been busy."

Leon grunted. "We'll be busy again if those Bugs decide to turn around and come back. How many troops you say you've got?"

"I haven't counted lately," the Stilter said coolly. "However, they're rallying to the colors in satisfying numbers." One armored manipulative member waved. "Are you in command of this deathtrap?"

Leon frowned. "Me and Retief been making most of the decisions," he said flatly. "I'm no general, if that's what you mean."

"Retief?" the Stilter's oculars swiveled. "Which one is he?"

Leon jerked a thumb at him. "You called this place a deathtrap," he started. "What—"

"Later," the biped said quickly, looking at Retief. "I thought—I understood he was a diplomat . . ."

"There are times when the wiliest diplomacy seems inadequate," Retief said. "This appeared to be one of them."

"I'd like to speak to you—in private," the Stilter said, sounding breathless.

"Hey, Retief, better watch this character—"

"It's all right, Leon," Retief said. He indicated an uncrowded spot a few feet distant. The Stilter stepped to it, then went on, paused inside the doorway to a building the roof of which was burning briskly, turned and faced Retief. The two upper arms went to the scarlet head, fumbled for a moment—

The mask lifted off, to reveal an oval face with wide blue eyes, a cascade of strawberry blond hair, a brilliant smile.

"Don't . . . don't you know me?" the girl almost wailed as Retief studied her approvingly. "I'm Fifi!"

Retief shook his head slowly. "Sorry—and I do mean sorry—"

"It's been quite a few years," the girl said appealingly, "but I thought . . ."

"You couldn't be over twenty-one," Retief said. "It would take more than twenty-one years to forget that face."

The girl tossed her head, her eyes sparkling. "Perhaps you'll recall the name Fianna Glorian . . . ?"

Retief's eyes widened. "You mean *little* Fifi . . . ?"

The girl clapped her gauntleted hands together, eliciting a loud clang. "Cousin Jame—I thought I'd *never* find you . . . !"

11

"I don't get it," Big Leon declared. "I turn my back for five minutes to see how the wounded are making out, and this Tief-tief character disappears back into the brush—and this little lady pops out of no place!"

"Not exactly no place, Mr. Caracki," Fifi corrected gently. "I was with the army."

"Yeah—and how you got there beats me; I've lived out here forty years and it's the first time—"

"I told you about the yacht crashing—"

"Sure—and then you bust out of a Voion jail and a couple Phips take you in hand—"

"The little green ones? They're cute!" Fifi said. "They led us to the Herpp village and told us about the rebel army—"

"Hey, Leon," a bearded Terran came up, gave Fifi an admiring look. "Looks like they're getting set for one more push before full dark—and this time they'll make it."

Leon growled. "The reinforcements are nice," he said. "But not enough. Them Bugs will be all over us like army ants in a few minutes. Sorry you had to get into this, young lady. I wish there was some way to smuggle you out of here—"

138

"Don't fret, Mr. Carnacki," Fifi said coolly. "I have a weapon." She held up an efficient-looking short-sword. "I wouldn't dream of missing the action."

"Hmmm . . . That looks like the one that Bug Tief-tief was carrying . . ."

"He gave it to me."

Leon grunted, turned away to bark an order. Retief leaned close to Fifi.

"You still haven't told me how you managed to take over my army."

"After I got the other girls settled in the native village, the little Phip led me to your scare-suit," Fifi whispered. "Of course, I didn't know whose it was, but I thought it would be a good disguise. As soon as I got it on, the Phips flew off buzzing like mad. The next thing I knew, there were Quoppina arriving from every direction. They seemed to accept me as their general, and I just went along . . ."

"You seemed to be playing the role to the hilt when I first caught sight of you, Fifi."

"I've listened to enough war stories to know a little tactics—which is more than can be said for the Voion."

A sharp hubbub broke out nearby; Retief stepped out to see Jik-jik, Tupper, several other Zilk and Ween, a pair of heavy Jackoo, half a dozen Herpp and a cluster of blue and white Clute and high-wheeled Blang, striking in lemon accented with orange polka dots.

"Where our war chief?" Jik-jik shrilled. "I wants to see Tief-tief, and I means now!"

"Steady, troops," Retief soothed. "Here I am."

"What you mean, here I is?" Jik-jik yelped. "I looking for a fighting Quopp name of Tief-tief, not some foreign-type Terry!"

"Shhh. I'm in disguise. Don't give me away."

"Oh." Jik-jik looked Retief over carefully. "Pretty good," he said in a conspiratorial tone. "Almost fooled me."

"Is it you, Tief?" Tupper hooted. "I feared ye were dead, the way ye dropped out of sight."

"Just a tricky bit of undercover work," Retief assured the group.

"Things is got worse since we seen you last," Jik-jik said. "Voion using new stuff on us!"

"Them Voion throwing thunderbolts now, for sure!" a Ween said. "Come nigh to melting my tail wheel down!" He displayed the two-inch coaster depending from the tip of his anterior segment.

"Hoo! It melted half away!" Jik-jik looked at Retief. "What this mean, War Chief?"

"It means the Federated Tribes are in trouble," he said. "The Voion are using guns."

"Where'd they get these whatchacallums, guns?" a Clute inquired. "I ain't never hear of nothing like that before. Melt a fellow down before he gets in harpoon range."

"I'm afraid there's been some meddling in Quopp's internal affairs," Retief said. "After we've cured the Voion of their interest in governing the planet, we'll have to reverse that trend." He looked over the delegation.

"I see you've picked up a few recruits. How did you manage it?"

"Well, Tief-tief," Jik-jik announced. "I got to thinking about my uncle Lub-lub and some of them other Ween in the next village, so I bribed a Phip to scatter over there and invite 'em to join the party. Seem like word got around, because volunteers done been coming in all day. Them Voion sure is got a heap of folks riled up at 'em."

"Nice work, Jik-jik—you, too, Tupper."

"What about me?" Fufu demanded. "While I was out on patrol, I caught a nosy Voion creeping up on us and flattened him single-wheeled!"

"Way I heard it, you was sneaking off the back way and run into the whole Voion army," Fut-fut commented. "It scare you so bad you come rolling back fast!"

"The idea! I'd just slipped away for a little solitary contemplation—"

"We'll compose a suitable military history of the operation later," Retief interposed. "We'll put in all the things we wish we'd done, and leave out the embarrassing mistakes. For now, we'll stick to practical politics."

"Ain't nothing practical about the fix us in," Jik-jik stated. "Us done cut our way right into a trap. They is got us outnumbered a six of sixes to one or I is a Voob's nephew."

"I resent that, you!" a small red-orange Quoppina said cockily, snapping a couple of medium-sized claws at the Ween. "We Voob—"

"Even you Voob can see they packed together out there like grubs in a brood-rack—"

"Watch y'r language, ye Wormless cannibal—" a Zilk grated.

"No bickering," Retief broke in. "Tonight we're all Quoppina together, or tomorrow we'll all be spare parts!"

It was full dark now. A pale glow in the south announced the imminent appearance of Joop. A Phip, its tiny pale green running lights glowing, dropped in, rotors whining, to settle on Retief's outstretched arm.

"Ween-ween set-set," it reported in a penny-whistle chirp. "Zilk-zilk chop-chop, Flink-flink swing-swing!"

"All right, we're as ready as we'll ever be," Retief said softly to Jik-jik, standing by with the other members of the general staff, one from each of the tribes now represented in the Federation, plus Leon, Fifi, and Seymour.

Retief swung up onto Fufu's back. "Leon, wait until our diversion has penetrated as far as the edge of the jungle; then hit them with all the firepower we've got. With a little luck, they might panic and pull out."

"And if a Dink had rotors, he wouldn't spin his wheels so much," a Blang muttered.

"All right, you Quoppina in the commando party; don't do anything brave and don't get captured," Retief directed. "Just stick to the plan and try to cause as much confusion as possible."

"Let's go," a Flink mounted astride a Jackoo whined. "Already nervous prostitution I got."

"All right—roll out!" Fufu huffed and started forward, rolling over a mat of flattened Voion, bursting out through the broached fence, sending Voion flying. Ahead, the suddenly aroused enemy were closing in, clubs waving and here and there the wink of a power gun, firing with wild inaccuracy.

Retief crouched over Fufu's neck, his sword held extended low on the right side. A Voion darted into his path, raised a gun—and slammed back as the point took him under the chest-plates. Another level a spear, jumped aside in the nick of time as Fufu thundered past, the others of the assault column close behind.

"Those city wheels," Fufu snorted. "No good at all for this sort of thing!" A Voion dashing to firing position

141

among the trees ahead threw up his arms, arced gracefully up into the air, paused, started a return swing, suspended by the neck from a length of purple rope. Another veered suddenly as a filmy net dropped to engulf him, went head over wheels in a cloud of dead leaves, tripping a pair of comrades.

"Those Flink are a caution," Fufu panted. "Shall I head back out now?"

"Affirmative—and look out for that big fellow with the harpoon—"

Fufu honked, swerved as a long barb-headed spear shot past his head, clattered off his side.

"Tief-tief, are you all right?" he shouted.

"Sure; nice dodging!" The Jackoo curving back now, racing through the trees for the shelter of the stockade. Behind him, Voion non-coms shrilled commands; a steady fire slashed after the retreating heavyweights. Fufu shied as a beam flicked across his flank, shifted into high gear.

"Yiiiii!" he bucked wildly. "That *stings!*"

Retief looked back; a pack of Voion were in close pursuit; light winked as they fired at the run, keeping to the six foot trail flattened by Fufu's hasty passage. More Voion packed the way ahead. Fufu plowed into the press, dozing the hapless Planetary forces aside like Indian clubs—but more popped up to fill their places.

"I'm getting . . . winded," the heavy mount called back over his shoulder. "There are so many of them . . ."

"Break it off, Fufu," Retief came back. "Looks like we can't make the stockade; we'll take to the woods and harass their flanks . . ."

"I'll try—but . . . I'm almost . . . pooped . . ."

"As soon as you hit the edge of the jungle, we'll form up a defensive ring," Retief called. He countered a swinging club in the grip of a Voion, ducked under a spear thrust, leaned aside from the flare of a power gun. Behind him, the other Jackoo of the detachment were in similar straits, hemmed in from all sides by a crushing press of Voion, those behind forcing the front rank unwillingly under the flattening treads of the heavy creatures.

"We'll form a circle," he shouted back to them. "Close spacing, and heads facing out; you Flink dismount and beat them off as long as you can!"

At the edge of the jungle now, Fufu wheezed to a halt;

Bubu came alongside, wheeled to face the forward-surging enemy; the others quickly took up positions to complete the ring. The oncoming Voion met wild swings from the embattled Jackoo's digging members, supported by vigorous resistance from Flink-wielded clubs and spears, captured from the Voion. Retief wrenched a power gun from the grip of a Voion who had managed to evade Fufu's shovel-tipped arms, blasted him with it, then downed another. A heap of damaged Voion grew around the tiny fortress; now the Voion attackers were forced to scale a mound of casualties to fire down into the enclosure.

Beside Retief, one Flink after another yelled, toppled backward, smoking from a hit. The few remaining rebels had all captured guns now; they fired steadily, but nearly as inaccurately as the Voion. Retief picked off one attacker after another, while the weapon grew hot in his hand. Then it buzzed dolefully and died. A Voion above him took aim, and Retief threw the gun, saw it clang off the Voion's armored head, knocking him backward—

There was a sudden change in the quality of the sounds of conflict: a high, thin shriek cut through the squalling of the Voion and the crackle of gunfire and fiercely burning metallo-wood. Dust rose in a swirl; a miniature tornado seemed to press at the crowded Voion, then hurl them backward—

Into the cleared patch thus created, something vast and dark slammed down with a ground-shaking impact, a boom! like a falling cliff. In the stunned silence that followed, pieces rattled down all around as shrill Voion cries rang out. Dust rolled away to show the pulverized remains of a Rhoon scattered across the field among windrows of felled Voion. A second huge dark shape appeared, beating across the scene of battle at low level, rotors hammering. The bright flash of a power gun winked above its lights.

"That does it, Tief-tief," Ozzl gasped. "Who could fight lightning from the sky?"

Something dropped from the Rhoon's underside, slammed down among the Voion, bounced high, hit again, cutting a swathe through ranks still stunned by the crash of the first of the giant creatures.

"Tief-tief!" a vast voice boomed, floating across the sky as the Rhoon lifted. "Tief-tief . . ."

143

"Listen!" Ozzl choked. "He's—he's calling you? What could it mean?"

Retief jumped up on Fufu's broad back. All around, the Voion were breaking and fleeing now, while the steady crackle and *bzzapp!* of power guns sounded from the vast dark shadows hanging above on hammering rotors.

"It means the fight's over!" Retief shouted above the hurricane. "It's Gertie and her friends with reinforcements from the city—and two hundred smuggled power pistols!"

An hour later, in an unburned room of the battered post office, Retief and his victorious allies sat around a wide table, sampling Terran trade rum, Bacchus brandy, and Quoppina Hellrose, cut three to one to stretch.

"Those blasters turned the trick, all right, Retief," Leon said. "What sleeve did you have them up?"

"Oh, they were stored conveniently in the customs shed. I hoped we wouldn't have to use them, but once the Voion started it, there wasn't much choice."

"You're a funny kind of diplomat, if you don't mind my mentioning it," Seymour commented. "I mean, sending Gertie to collect contraband guns so you could blast the government army—it was a neat move, don't get me wrong—but what'll Longspoon say?"

"Actually, Seymour, I hadn't intended to tell him."

"I hope all of you gentlemen will display the most complete discretion," Fifi said sweetly. "Otherwise, I'll come gunning for you personally."

"Retief did what he had to do," Leon growled. "What good's a dead diplomat?"

"That's a question we'd better not examine too closely," Retief said. "And since we're now in position to present the authorities with a *fait accompli,* I don't think anyone will pursue it to its logical conclusion."

"You is got my guarantee," Jik-jik announced. "The new Federated Tribes ain't going ask no embarrassing questions."

A Terran planter thrust his head into the room. "The Bugs—*our* Bugs, I mean—just brought in the Voion general. Ugly-looking little devil. What do you think we ought to do with him?"

"Retief, you want to talk to this Jasper?" Leon demanded. "Or should I just throw him back?"

"Maybe I'd better have a word with him." Retief and Fifi followed Leon along to the room where the captive Voion huddled on splayed wheels, his drooping antennae expressive of profound dejection. One ocular twitched as he saw Retief.

"Let me talk to him—alone," he squeaked in a weak voice. Retief nodded. Leon frowned at him.

"Every time somebody gets you off to the side, funny things start happening, Retief; I've got an idea you're not telling all you know."

"Just my diplomatic reflex, Leon. I'll be with you in five minutes."

"Watch that bird; he many have a spare sticker under his inlay."

As soon as the two Terrans had left, the Voion lifted off his headpiece to reveal the pale gray visage of General Hish.

"To give you credit, Terry," he hissed in Groaci. "To have sucked me in neatly with the pretense of disorganization."

"Don't feel too badly, General; if you only knew how I labored over the timing—"

"To not forget the miserable quality of the troops under my command," Hish added anxiously. "To wish the lot of them disassembled and exported—" He broke off. "But I tire you with these recriminations," he went on smoothly in Voion. "Now, as a fellow member of a foreign mission, I assume you'll accord me the usual courtesies . . ."

Retief looked thoughtful. "Let me see; as far as I can recall, the courtesies I received the last time I was a guest of the Groaci—"

"Now, now, my dear Retief, we mustn't hold grudges, eh? Just give me an escort to my heli and we'll let bygones be bygones—"

"There are a few little points I'd like for you to clear up for me first," Retief said. "You can start by telling me what the Groaci Foreign Office had in mind when it started arming the Voion."

Hish made a clicking noise indicating surprise. "But my dear chap—I thought it was common knowledge that it was your own Ambassador Longspoon who conceived the notion of supplying, ah, educational material . . . ?"

"Terry power guns make a blue flash, Hish," Retief said patiently. "Those of Groaci manufacture make yellow ones —even when they're tricked out with plastic covers to look like Terry guns. It was one of your flimsier deceptions—"

"Speaking of deceptions," Hish mused, "I feel sure your own clever impersonation will cause quite a stir among your troops, once it's known—to say nothing of the reaction among your colleagues when they discover you've been leading an armed insurrection—and against your own CDT-supported faction at that."

"It might—if there were anyone alive who knew about it—and felt gabby," Retief agreed.

"I'm alive," Hish pointed out. "And while 'gabby' is not perhaps the word I would have employed—"

"There's not much I can do about your gabbiness," Retief cut in. "But as for your being alive—"

"Retief! You wouldn't? Not a fellow alien! A fellow diplomat! A fellow illegal operator!"

"Oh, I might," Retief said. "Now, suppose you demonstrate that gabbiness you were boasting about a few seconds ago . . ."

". . . in the strictest confidence," Hish croaked, mopping at his throat sac with a large green hanky. "If Ambassador Schluh ever suspected—that is, if he knew of my professional confidences—"

There was a scrape of feet outside the door. Hish hastily donned his head as the yellow-bearded Terran came into the room. "Hey, Mr. Retief," he said. "There's a fellow out here just made a sloppy landing in a heli. Says he's from the Terry Embassy at Ixix. Leon says you better talk to him."

"Certainly," Retief got to his feet. "Where is he?"

"Right here . . ." the blond man motioned. A second figure appeared in the door—muddy, tattered, his clothing awry, his cheeks unshaven; Leon, Fifi, Seymour, and a crowd of others were behind him.

"Retief!" Magnan gasped. "Then you—how—I thought —but never mind. They let me go—that is, they sent me —Ikk sent me—"

"Maybe you'd better sit down and collect yourself, Mr. Magnan," Retief put a hand under the First Secretary's elbow, guided him to a chair. Magnan sank down.

"He has them—all of us—the entire staff," he choked. "From Ambassador Longspoon—locked up in his own Chancery, mind you—down to the merest code clerk! And unless the Federated Tribes instantly lay down their arms, disband their army, and release all prisoners, he's going to hang them right after breakfast tomorrow!"

"All I got to say is," Seymour announced, hitching up his pants, "we ain't about to give up what we won just to save a bunch of CDT slickers from a necktie party. Serves 'em right for chumming up to them Voion in the first place."

"Retief didn't ask you to," Big Leon snapped. "Shut up, Seymour. Anyway, we didn't win the fight—the Bugs did."

"But the sixty-one prisoners," Magnan protested breathlessly. "Twenty women—"

"Longspoon ought to appreciate being strung up by his pals," a man put in. "Those Quopp tribesmen will sure do the job if the Voion don't."

"It's a tough deal," Leon cut in. "But even if we went along, we got no guarantee Ikk wouldn't hang 'em anyway—and us alongside of 'em."

"I'm afraid doing business with Ikk is out of the question," Retief agreed. "The former prime minister is one of those realistic souls who never let a matter of principle stand in the way of practical matters. Still, I think hanging the whole staff is a bit severe."

"He must be out of his mind," someone said. "He'll have a couple squadrons of CDT Peace Enforcers in here before you can say Jack Dools—"

"Ikk is an end-of-the-world type," Retief said. "He's not concerned about consequences—not until they jump out and grab him by the back of the neck."

"I say let's get the Bug army together—"

"The Federated Tribes," Retief corrected gently.

"Yeah—OK, the Federated Tribes. We march 'em straight through to Ixix, with plenty of Rhoon cover, take over the town, kick out the Voion garrison, tell old Ikk to hang up his toolbox, and put in a call for CDT Monitors—"

"CDT Monitors, hell," Seymour growled. "What did the CDT ever do for Quopp except give the Voion big ideas?"

"Gentlemen, it's apparent that the next target for the

147

Federation is the capital," Retief said. "I want you to wait one day before starting, however."

"Hell, let's hit 'em now, before they get a chance to pull themselves together—"

"That ain't likely—not with their general cooling his wheels here." Seymour nodded toward Hish, sitting silently in a corner.

"What you want us to wait for, Retief?" Les demanded.

"Don't sound any dumber'n you got to," Big Leon growled. "He needs a few hours to try to spring the ambassador and his rappies before Ikk strings 'em up." He looked at Retief. "Seymour and me'll go with you."

"Three Terries would be just a trifle too conspicuous in Ixix tonight," Retief said. "But I think I'll take our friend the general along for company."

Hish jumped as though stung by a zinger. "Why me?" he whispered.

"You'll be my guide," Retief said blandly.

"How do you figure to make your play?" Leon asked.

"There are a few supplies I'll need. Then I'll have to go over to the Federation camp and talk to the local headmen," Retief said. "We'll work out something."

Leon looked at him with narrowed eyes. "There's angles to this I'm not getting," he said. "But that's OK. I guess you know what you're doing."

Fifi put a hand on his arm. "Jame—have you really got to . . . ? But that's a stupid question, isn't it?" She managed a smile. Retief put a finger under her chin.

"Better send out some Jackoo and an escort and get the girls in here to camp and ready to march. Tomorrow night you'll all be celebrating with a big party aboard a Corps Transport."

"But we c-came to see *you* . . . !"

"You will," Retief said. "I claim the first dance."

"Yeah," Shorty said under his breath. "Let's hope he's got both feet on the floor when he gets it."

12

With his Quoppina armor in an inconspicuous bundle under one arm and Hish, still in Voion trappings, trailing dismally, Retief followed a guiding Phip to the Ween encampment a mile from Rum Jungle. Startled veterans of the morning's action jumped up, fighting claws ready, as he walked into the clearing around their main campfire, the Groaci close on his heels. Jik-jik came forward.

"Well, you must be one of them Terries us saved the bacon for," he shrilled, coming up close. "Hmmm; you looks tender and juicy . . ."

"We've already been through this routine, Jik-jik," Retief said in a low voice. "Don't you know me?"

"Oh, uh, yeah," Jik-jik made a fast recovery. "Well, Terry, just step on in and sit down. Just be a little bit careful one of the boys don't get kind of curious and nip off a small bite."

"I'm poison," Retief said loudly. "You get terrible belly cramps if you eat a Terry, and afterward your cuticula falls off in big patches." He took a seat on a fallen log; Hish hovered close, looking nervously at the Ween fighting claws gleaming all around. "I have to get into town, Jik-

149

jik," Retief said. "I'm going to need some help from the tribes with what I have in mind . . ."

Retief, once again clad in his bright-colored armor, scanned the ground below as the immense male Rhoon on which he rode beat its way southward in company with a dozen picked companions. To the left flew the steed of General Hish, a mount specially equipped with a dummy cockpit astride which the terrified Groaci sat, a gay red scarf fluttering from his neck. "It looks as though the ground troops have rounded up most of the refugees from last night's fiasco," Retief called to his Rhoon. "I see a few small parties huddled together here and there, but no concentrations."

"Except the fifty thousand of the rascals who still behind the city's towers hide," the deep voice boomed. "My hope it is they'll venture up, their stolen Rhoonish corpses to employ against us."

"I doubt if you'll get your wish," Retief said. "Gerthudion and her friends have pretty well cleared the skies, I think."

With the Rhoon carrying Hish a hundred yards in advance, Retief's flyer descended steadily, passed over the port at five hundred feet, aiming for the rooftop heli pad that crowned the Terran Chancery Tower.

"That gun crew down there is tracking us," Retief said. "But they're not quite sure enough to shoot."

"That's but a trivial hazard, Tief-tief, compared with challenging the Blackwheel's stronghold."

"Let's hope Hish remembers his lines."

"The prospect of Lundelia's rending claws will him inspire to a flawless performance," the Rhoon croaked. Ahead, the lead Rhoon settled in to the pad, Hish clinging to his saddle, his jaunty scarf fluttering downward now in the air blast from Lundelia's rotors. Two Voion posted on the roof rolled to meet him, guns in hand. Hish lowered himself awkwardly, cast a nervous glance at the looming head of his mount; his arms waved as he spoke to the police. He pointed to Retief's Rhoon, now dropping in to light beside Lundelia. The big flyer braked his rotors to a stop with a final whop-whop-woooppp of displaced air.

". . . prisoner," Hish was whispering. "Just stand aside, fellow, and I'll take him along to His Omnivoracity."

As Retief jumped down, Hish waved the power gun from which the energy cell had been removed. "I'm sure the prime minister will be interested in meeting the rebel chieftain, Tief-tief," he amplified.

"So that's the bandit, eh?" One of the Voion rolled over, peering through the failing light of the sun, now a baleful spotlight behind flat purple clouds on the horizon. "He's a queer-looking Quopp; how'd you snare him?"

"I snatched him single-handed from under the noses of his compatriots, killing dozens and injuring hundreds more," Hish snapped in his breathy Groaci voice. "Now clear my path before I lose my temper and add you to the list of casualties."

"OK, OK, don't get huffy," the guard said sullenly. He waved the pair toward the door. "For your sake I hope that's the genuine article you've got there," he muttered as Hish rolled awkwardly by on his prosthetic wheels.

"Oh, I'm genuine," Retief said. "You don't think he'd lie to you?"

Inside, Retief went ahead of Hish, glanced along the short hall, turned to Hish.

"You're doing fine, General. Now don't get excited and blow this next scene; it's the climax of the morning's entertainment." He took the gun, fitted the kick-stick back in the butt, slipped it into his concealed hip holster, then adjusted his face mask.

"How do I look?"

"Like an insomniac's nightmare," Hish whispered. "Let me go now, Retief! When you're shot down for the idiot you are, it would be a pity if I were caught in the overkill."

"I'll see that your passing won't be accidental," Retief reassured the Groaci. He checked to see that the bulky pouch slung over his left hip was in place; its contents shifted with a dull clank of glass.

"All right, Hish," he said. "Let's go down."

"How can I negotiate these stairs, wheeled as I am?" the Groaci demanded.

"No stalling, General; just bump down the way the Voion do, not forgetting to use the handrails."

Hish complied, grumbling. In the wide corridor one flight down, Voion sentries posted at intervals turned cold oculars on the pair.

"Sing pretty," Retief said softly.

"You there," Hish keened at the nearest Voion. "Which are the chambers of His Omnivoracity?"

"Who wants to know, wobbly-wheels?" the cop came back. "What's this you've got in tow? A terry-Quopp half-breed?" He made the scratchy sound that indicated Appreciation of One's Own Wit.

"What wandering cretin fertilized your tribal ovum racks just prior to your hatching?" Hish inquired pointedly. "But I waste time with these pleasantries. Show me the way to the prime minister or I'll see to it your component parts are added to the bench stock in a front line reppo deppo."

"You will, eh? Who the Worm you think you are—"

Hish tapped his narrow, Voion-armored thorax with a horny pseudoclaw, eliciting a hollow clunk. "Is it possible you don't know the insignia of a general officer?" he hissed.

"Uh—is that what you are?" the fellow hesitated. "I never saw one—"

"That omission has now been rectified," Hish announced. "Quickly now! This prisoner is the insurgent commander-in-chief!"

"Yeah?" The guard rolled closer. Others in hearing pricked up their auditory antennae, moving in to follow the conversation.

"To watch your step," Retief said quietly in Groaci. "To remember that if I have to shoot, you'll be in my line of fire . . ."

"Stop!" Hish snapped hoarsely, waving back the curious Voion. "Resume your posts at once! Clear the way—"

"Let's have a look at this Stilter," a Voion shrilled.

"Yeah, I'd like to get a piece of the Quopp that blew the wheels off a couple of former associates of mine!"

"Let's work him over!"

Hish crowded back against Retief. "One step closer, and you die!" he choked. "I can assure you a gun is aimed at your vitals at this instant—"

"I don't see any guns—"

"Let's see if this Stilter's arms bend—"

There was the crash of a door slamming wide, an ear-splitting screech of Voion rage; the sentries whirled to see the oversized figure of Prime Minister Ikk, Jarweel feathers atremble with rage, confronting them, flanked by armed guards.

"You pond scum have the unmitigated insolence to conduct a free-for-all at my very door?" he shrilled. "I'll have the organ-clusters off the lot of you! Niv! Kuz! Shoot them down where they stand!"

"Ah . . . if I might interject a word, Your Omnivoracity . . . ?" Hish raised a hand. "I hope you remember me —General Hish? I just happened along with my prisoner—"

"Hish? Prisoner? What—" The irate leader clacked his jeweled palps with a sound like a popped paper bag, staring at the disguised Groaci. "You mentioned the name of, ah, General Hish . . ."

"Ah—there was the matter of a suitable, er, cover identity . . . ?"

"Cover . . ." Ikk rolled up, waving the chastened sentries aside. He stared closely at Hish. "Hmmm. Yes," he muttered. "I see the joints now; nice job. You look like a tribal reject with axle rickets and shorted windings, but I'd never have guessed . . ." He looked at Retief. "And this is a prisoner, you say, Hish?"

"This, my dear Ikk, is the leader of the rabble forces."

"What—are you sure?" Ikk rolled quickly back, looking Retief up and down. "I heard he was a Stilter . . . maroon cuticula . . . rudimentary rotors . . . by the Worm, it fits! How did you manage—but never mind! Bring him along!" He whirled; his eye fell on the sentries huddled in a clump under the watchful oculars of the bodyguards.

"Send these good fellows along," he shrilled merrily. "See that they all get promotions. Nothing like a show of spirit, I always say. Shows morale's up." Buzzing a merry tune, the Voion leader led the way through the wide door into the ambassadorial office, took up his pose under the large portrait of himself hanging where the Corps Ensign had been on Retief's last visit.

"Now," he rubbed his grasping members together, eliciting a sound effect reminiscent of a hacksaw cutting an oil drum. "Let's have a look at the dacoit who had the effrontery to imagine he could interfere with my plans!"

"Ah, Ikk," Hish made a fluttery gesture. "There are

aspects to the present situation I haven't yet mentioned . . ."

"Well?" Ikk canted his oculars at the Groaci. "Mention them at once! Not that they can be of any importance, with this fellow in my hands. A capital piece of work, Hish! For this, I may allow you to . . . But we'll go into that later."

"It's rather private," Hish whispered urgently. "If you wouldn't mind sending these fellows along . . .?"

"Umph." Ikk waved an arm at his bodyguards. "Get out, you two. And while you're at it, tell Sergeant Uzz and his carpenters to hurry up with the ten-Terry gibbet. No need to wait until morning now."

The two Voion rolled silently to the door, closed it gently behind them. Ikk turned to Retief, making a clattering sound with his zygomatic plates indicative of Pleasure Anticipated.

"Now, criminal," he purred. "What have you to say for yourself?"

Retief lifted the holster flap, snapped out the power gun and leveled it at Ikk's head. "I'll let this open the conversation," he said genially.

Ikk crouched, slumped down over his outward-slanting wheels, his lower arms slack, his upper pair picking nervously at his chest inlays.

"You!" he addressed Hish. "A traitor! I trusted you! I gave you full powers, listened to your counsels, turned over my army to you! And now this!"

"Surprising how these matters sometimes turn out," Hish agreed in his whispery voice. He had his headpiece off now and was smoking one of Ikk's imported dopesticks. "Of course, there was the little matter of the assassins assigned to eliminate me from the picture as soon as you had achieved your modest goal, but of course that was to be expected."

Ikk's oculars twitched. "Who, me?" he said dazedly. "Why . . ."

"Naturally, I eliminated them the first day; a small needle fired into their main armatures did the trick neatly—"

There was a small sound at the door; it snapped wide and Ikk's two bodyguards rolled quickly through, guns at the ready, flipped the door shut behind them. Ikk came to life then, dropped behind the platinum ambassadorial desk as the two swiveled to face Hish. Behind the Groaci, Retief held the gun steady against his hostage's backplates.

"Shoot them down, Kuz!" Ikk shrilled. "Blast them into atoms! Burn them where they stand; never mind about the rug . . ." His voice faded off. He extended an ocular above tabletop level, saw the two Voion standing, guns at their sides.

"What's this?" he shrilled. "I order you to shoot them at once!"

"Please, my dear Ikk!" Hish objected. "Those supersonic harmonics are giving me a splitting headache!"

Ikk rose up, his palps working spasmodically. "But—but I summoned them! I pushed my secret button right here under my green and pink inlay . . ."

"Of course. But naturally, your bodyguards are on my payroll. But don't feel badly; after all, my budget—"

"But—" Ikk waved his arms at the Voion. "You can't mean it, fellows! Traitors to your own kind?"

"They're a couple of chaps you ordered disassembled for forgetting to light your dope-stick," Hish said. "I countermanded the order and planted them on you. Now—"

"Then—at least let them shoot the Stilter!" Ikk proposed. "Surely you and I can settle our little differences—"

"The Stilter has the drop on me, I'm afraid, Ikk. No, these two good lads will have to be locked in the W.C. Attend to it, will you, there's a good fellow."

"You handled that properly, Hish," Retief commended as Ikk rolled dejectedly back after snapping the lock behind his former adherents. "Now, Ikk, I think we'd better summon Ambassador Longspoon here to make the party complete."

Ikk grumbled, pressed a button on the silver mounted call box, snapped an order. Five minutes dragged past. There was a tap at the door.

"You'll know just how to handle this," Retief suggested gently to the prime minister.

Ikk twitched his oculars. "Send the Terry in!" he snapped. "Alone!"

The door opened cautiously; a sharp nose appeared past its edge, then an unshaven, receding chin, followed by the rest of the Terran ambassador. He ducked his head at Ikk, shot a glance at Retief and Hish, whose face was again concealed behind the Voion mask. He let the door click behind him, tugged at the upper set of chrome-plated lapels of his mauve after-midnight extra-formal cutaway, incongruous in the early evening light that gleamed through the hexagonal window behind Ikk.

"Ahh . . . there you are, Mr. Prime Minister," he said. "Er, ah . . ."

"Hish, tell him not to get in my line of fire," Retief said in Tribal. Longspoon's eyes settled on Retief, still fully armored, jumped to the disguised Groaci, then back to the prime minister. "I'm not sure I understand . . ."

"The person behind me is armed, my dear Archie," Hish said. "I fear he, not our rspected colleague, the prime minister, controls the situation."

Longspoon stared blankly at Retief, his close-set eyes taking in the maroon chest-plates, the scarlet-dyed head, the pink rotors.

"Who—who is he?" he managed.

"He's the Worm-doomed troublemaker who's had the effrontery to defeat my army," Ikk snapped. "So much for visions of a Quopp united in Voionhood."

"And," Hish put in quickly, "you'll be astonished to learn that his name is . . ." He paused as though remembering something.

"Why, I know the bandit's name," Longspoon's mouth clamped in an indignant expression. "As a diplomat, it's my business to keep in touch with these folk movements. It's, ah, Tough-tough or Toof-toof or something of the sort."

"How clever of Your Excellency," Hish murmured.

"Now that the introductions are out of the way," Retief said in Tribal, "we'd better be getting on with the night's work. Ikk, I want the entire Embassy staff taken to the port and loaded aboard these foreign freighters you've impounded and permitted to lift. Meanwhile, we'll use the hot line to Sector HQ to get a squadron of CDT Peace Enforcers headed out this way. I hope they arrive in time to salvage a few undamaged Voion for use as museum specimens."

"What's he saying?" Longspoon pulled at his stiff vermillion collar, his mouth opening and closing as though he were pumping air over gills.

"He demands that you and your staff leave Quopp at once," Ikk said quickly.

"What's that? Leave Quopp? Abandon my post? Why, why, this is outrageous! I'm a fully accredited Terran emissary of Galactic Good Will! How could I ever explain to the under-secretary—"

"Tell him you departed under duress," Ikk suggested. "Driven out by lawless criminals wielding illegal firearms."

"Firearms? Here on Quopp? But that's . . . that's—"

"A flagrant violation of Interplanetary Law," Hish whispered piously. "Shocking . . ."

"Give the orders, Ikk," Retief said. "I want the operation concluded before Second Jooprise. If I have to sit here any longer with my finger on the firing stud it may begin to twitch involuntarily."

"What? What?" Longspoon waited for a translation.

"He threatens to kill me unless I do as he commands," Ikk said. "Much as I regret seeing you depart under such ah, humiliating circumstances, Archie, I fear I've no choice. Still, after your dismissal from the Corps for gross dereliction of duty in permitting shipments of Terry-manufactured arms to the rebels—"

"I? Nonsense! There are no Terran weapons on Quopp—"

"Look at the gun even now being aimed at my Grand Cross of the Legion d'Cosme," Ikk snapped. "I assume you know a Terran power pistol when it's pointed between your eyes!"

Longspoon's face sagged. "A Browning Mark XXX," he gasped.

Hish canted an eye to look at Retief. Retief said nothing.

"Still," Ikk went on, "you can always write your memoirs—under a pseudonym of course, the name Longspoon having by then acquired a Galaxy-wide taint—"

"I'll not go!" Longspoon's Adam's apple quivered with indignation. "I'll stay here until this is covered up—or, rather, until I'm able to clarify the situation!"

"Kindly advise the ambassador that his good friend Ikk intends to hang him," Retief instructed Hish.

"Lies!" Ikk screeched in Terran. "All lies! Archie and I have sucked the Sourball of Eternal Chumship!"

"I'll not stir an inch!" Longspoon quavered. "My mind is made up!"

"Let's have a little action, Ikk," Retief ordered. "I can feel the first twitch coming on."

"You wouldn't dare," Ikk keened faintly. "My loyal troops would tear you wheel from wheel . . ."

"But you won't be here to see it." Prodding Hish ahead of him, Retief went up to the desk, leaned on it, put the gun to Ikk's central inlay. "Now," he said.

Behind him there was a rustle, a wheeze of effort—

He stepped back, whirled in time to see a chair wielded by the ambassador an instant before it crashed down across his head.

"Ah," Ikk purred, like a knife sawing through corn husks. "Our rabble-rouser is now in position to see matters in a new light . . ." He made rattling noises in tribute to the jest. Retief, strapped into the same chair with which Longspoon had crowned him, many loops of stout cord restraining his arms, held his headpiece half turned away from the lamp which had been placed to glared into his oculars. A pair of heavy-armed Voion interrogation specialists stood by, implements ready. Hish was parked in a corner, striving to appear inconspicuous. Longspoon, his lapels awry, hooked a finger under the rope knotted about his neck.

"I . . . I don't understand, Your Omnivoracity," he quavered. "What's the nature of the ceremony I'm to take part in?"

"I promised you'd be elevated to a high post," Ikk snapped. "Silence, or we'll settle for a small informal ritual right here in your office." He rolled over to confront Retief. "Who supplied the nuclear weapons with which you slaughtered my innocent, fun-loving, primitively armed freedom fighters? The Terrans, no doubt? A classic double cross."

"The Terrans supplied nothing but big ideas," Retief confided, "and you Voion got all those."

"A claw-snap for their ideas." Ikk clicked his claws

158

in discharge of the obligation. "You imagine I intended to conduct the planet's business with a cold Terran nose in all my dealings, carping at every trifling slum-clearance project that happened to involve the disassembly of a few thousand Sub-Voion villagers? Hah! Longspoon very generously supplied sufficient equipment to enable me to launch the Liberation; his usefulness ended the day the black banner of United Voionhood went up over Ixix!" He turned back to Retief. "Now, you will at once supply full information on rebel troop dispositions, armaments, unit designations—"

"Why ask him about troop dispositions, Ikk?" one of the interrogators asked. "Every Quopp on the planet's headed this way; we won't have any trouble finding them—"

"It's traditional," Ikk snapped. "Now shut up and let me get on with this!"

"I thought we were the interrogators," the other Voion said sullenly. "You stick to your prime-ministering and let Union Labor do their job—"

"Hmmmph. I hope the Union will enter no objection if my good friend Hish assists with the chore in the capacity of technical adviser?" He canted an ocular at the disguised Groaci. "What techniques would you recommend as being the most fun as well as most effective?"

"Whom, I?" Hish stalled. "Why, wherever did you get an idea like that . . .?"

"To keep them occupied," Retief said quickly in Groaci. "To remember which side of the bread substitute has the ikky-wax on it."

"What's that?" Ikk waggled his antennae alertly at Retief. "What did you say?"

"Just invoking the Worm in her own language," Retief clarified.

"What language is that?"

"Worman, of course."

"Oh yes. Well, don't do it any more—"

"Ikk!" Hish exclaimed. "A most disturbing thought has just come to me . . ."

"Well, out with it." Ikk tilted his eyes toward the Groaci.

"Ah—er . . . I hardly know how to phrase it . . ."

Ikk rolled toward him. "I've yet to decide just how to

deal with you, Hish; I suggest you endear yourself to me immediately by explaining what these hems and haws signify!"

"I was thinking . . . that is, I hadn't thought . . . I mean, have you happened to think . . ."

Ikk motioned his torturers over. "I warn you, Hish— you'll tell me what this is all about at once, or I'll give my Union men a crack at some overtime!"

As Hish engaged the Voion in conversation, Retief twisted his arm inside the fitted armor sheath, slipped his hand free of the gauntlet; the confining rope fell away. He reached to the pouch still slung at his side, lifted the flap, took out a small jar of thick amber fluid.

"Awwwwkk!" Ambassador Longspoon pointed at him, eyes goggling. "Help! It's liquid smashite! He'll blow us all to atoms—"

Ikk and his troops spun on their wheels; one Voion scrabbled at a holster, brought up a gun as the jar arched through the air, smashed at his feet; a golden puddle spread across the rug in an aroma of pure Terran clover honey. There was a moment's stunned silence.

"Sh—shoot him!" Ikk managed. The Voion with the gun dropped the weapon, dived for the fragrant syrup; an instant later, both interrogators were jackknifed over the honey, quivering in ecstasy, their drinking organs buried in nectar a thousand times stronger than the most potent Hellrose. Ikk alone still resisted, his antennae vibrating like struck gongs. He groped, brought up a gun, wavered, dithered, then with a thin cry dropped it and dived for the irresistible honey.

Retief shook the ropes from his arms, undid the straps and stood.

"Well done, General," he said. "I think that concludes this unfortunate incident in Quopp history. Now you and I had better have that little private chat you mentioned earlier . . ."

13

It was almost dawn. Ambassador Longspoon, freshly shaved and arrayed in a crisp breakfast hour informal dickey in puce and ocher stripes, stared glumly across the width of his platinum desk at Retief, now back in mufti. Beside him, Colonel Underknuckle rattled a sheet of paper, cleared his throat, beetled his eyebrows.

"The report indicates that after the accused was seen with the bomb—just before being reported absent without leave—a cursory inspection of his quarters revealed, among other curiosities, the following: a dozen pairs of hand-tooled polyon undergarments with the monogram 'L,' absent for some weeks from the wardrobe of Your Excellency; three cases of aged Pepsi from the ambassadorial private stock; a voluminous secret correspondence with unnamed subversive elements; a number of reels of high-denomination credit reported missing from the Budget and Fiscal Office; and a collection of racy photos of unfertilized ova."

"Gracious," Magnan murmured. "Did you find all those things yourself, Fred?"

"Of course not," the military attaché snapped. "The Planetary Police turned them up."

161

"What's that?" Longspoon frowned. "Considering subsequent events, I hardly think we can enter *their* findings as evidence. Let's confine ourselves to the matter of the bomb, and the irregularities at the port—and of course, the AWOL."

"Hmmmph! Seems a pity to waste perfectly good evidence . . ."

"Mr. Ambassador," Magnan piped. "I'm sure it's all just an unfortunate misunderstanding. Perhaps Retief wasn't at the port at all . . ."

"Well?" Longspoon waited, eyes boring into Retief.

"I was there," Retief said mildly.

"But—but, maybe it wasn't really a bomb he had," Magnan offered.

"It was a bomb, all right," Retief conceded.

"Well, in that case," Longspoon began—

"Ah—gentlemen, if I may put in a word . . . ?" General Hish, minus his Voion trappings and dapper in a dun-colored hip-cloak and jeweled eye-shields, hitched his chair forward. "The bomb . . . ah . . . it was, er, that is to say, I, ah . . ."

"Yes, yes, get on with it, General," Longspoon snapped. "I've a number of other questions to ask you as soon as this distasteful business is cleared up."

"It was my bomb." Hish whispered.

"*Your* bomb?" Underknuckle and Longspoon said in chorus.

"I, ah, had been led astray by evil companions," Hish said, arranging his mandibles at angles indicative of deprecation. "That is, I had supplied the infernal machine to a group whom I understood intended to employ it to er, ah, carry out patriotic measures directed against reactionary elements. Little did I suspect that it was the Terran Embassy which was thus so ungenerously characterized. At the last moment, learning of the full intent of these insidious schemers, I, um, advised Mr. Retief of its whereabouts—"

"Heavens, nobly done!" Magnan gushed. "Gracious, and I always thought your Groaci had sort of a teentsy little prejudice against us Terrans."

"Ignoring for the moment the matter of Groaci interference in Quopp's internal affairs," Underknuckle barked, "there's still the matter of the stolen publications!

What about that, eh? Can't wiggle out of this one, can you, by golly!"

"Oh, I wanted to mention," Magnan said. "Those bound volumes of the *Pest Control Journal*—"

"You didn't say *Pest Control Journal*, did you, Magnan?" Longspoon demanded.

'Yes, indeed I did say *Pest Contr*—"

"What idiot shipped that particular periodical in here?" Longspoon bellowed. "The entire journal's devoted to methods of anihilating arthropods with chitinous exoskeletons and ventral ladder-type nervous systems! If that sort of thing were ever released among the Quoppina— why, we'd be hailed as the greatest murderers since Attila the Hung!"

"Hun," Magnan corrected.

"Well, I trust he was hung eventually! And the same goes for the nincompoop who ordered the PCJ!"

"Gee, Fred." Magnan looked at Underknuckle. "Wasn't it you who—"

"Well, so that's taken care of," Underknuckle said briskly.

"That seems to leave nothing outstanding but the unauthorized absence," Longspoon commented. "We can deal with this charge at the local level, I think, Fred."

"Pity, in a way." The attaché blinked at Retief. "I'd intended to ship him out under guard for examination by a Board of Interrogators, after which he'd be stripped of rank in a most colorful ceremony—"

The desk screen buzzed. "The Revolutionary Council is here to see you, Mr. Ambassador," a vinegary voice announced.

"Show them in at once, Fester." Longspoon arranged his features, faced the door expectantly. "I'll just quickly establish my ascendancy over these fellows," he explained. "May as well get matters off on the correct footing . . ."

Magnan leaned toward Retief. "I love watching him work," he murmured. "It only took hm an instant to decide on Hearty Congratulation plus Alert Awareness of Irregularities, and just the teeniest bit of Latent Severity, all tied together with a touch of Gracious Condescension."

"A great technician," Retief agreed. "Too bad you can't tell the result from Stunned Incredulity."

"Umm. Still, the Quoppina won't know the difference."

The door opened; Fester appeared, ushering in the newly buffed figure of Jik-jik, his scarlet-cuticula gleaming under multiple coats of wax, a new Jarweel feather bobbing behind his left rear antenna. Behind him was the tall figure of Tupper, similarly glorified; Ozzl followed, with half a dozen other representatives of the victorious Federation.

"Ah, Mr. Tief-tief, I presume?" Longspoon rose, extended a hand. Jik-jik waved it off.

"No thanks, not hungry. Besides, us is got a new rule: Greens for Grubs and Grown-ups. Allies is better than Entrées."

"What's he saying?" Longspoon muttered.

"He's just explaining the Federation's new dietary arrangements," Retief explained.

"A food faddist, eh?" Longspoon nodded wisely.

Jik-jik glanced about the room; his oculars settled on Retief. "Hey," he said. "Ain't you——"

"Still working under cover," Retief said quickly. "Pretend you don't know me."

"Tell Mr. Tief-tief that I'm much disturbed by the recent disorders," Longspoon instructed. "Still, I'll listen to an explanation."

"Did you get the Terry females into the city safely?" Retief asked the Ween.

"Sure did, Tief-tief; they at the port, waiting for that Terry Peace Enforcer coming in this morning."

"What did he say?" Longspoon demanded.

"He'll examine your credentials presently, Mr. Ambassador. Meanwhile, keep your manipulative members out of Quopp's affairs."

"He said *that*?" Longspoon's face darkened.

"I'm giving a free translation," Retief explained. "Meanwhile, what about CDT recognition of the new regime?"

"Recognition? Hmmm. There *was* the matter of a certain understanding with the Voion . . ."

"Shall I remind him of that?"

"By no means! Tell him, ah, that I shall look forward to regularization of relations between our two peoples as soon as one or two points are ironed out. Now, we'll want an understanding on commercial matters; I think a thousand-man Trade Mission would be about right . . ."

"Did you find the remains of the yacht the girls were in?" Retief inquired of Jik-jik.

"Uh-huh. Just like you say, Tief-tief: It blasted by some kind of big fire gun. Big hole busted in the side."

Retief glanced at Hish, who aimed his five eyes at different corners of the room, began humming the opening bars of *You Tell Me Your Dream, I'll Tell You Mine*.

"Well?" Longspoon barked.

"He says there's to be no Terry interference in Quopp's tradition of free enterprise," Retief advised the ambassador. "And no more harassment of the traders at Rum Jungle and the other market towns."

"Eh? But what about the land reform program . . . ?"

"There'll be a big party tonight aboard the Terry ship," Retief said to the delegates. "The ambassador hopes you can make it."

"Nothing like a little socializing to take the boys' mind off the fun they missing not getting to loot the town," Jik-jik said. "Us'll be there."

"The Federated Tribes will tolerate no political intervention of any kind," Retief relayed to Longspoon. "They specifically reject anything with the word 'reform' in it."

"Gad! This fellow's a reactionary of the worst stripe! Surely he won't object to my Jungle Slum clearance plan, my Pretties for the Underprivileged Program, and my Spiraling Price Support formula—"

"I hope you followed my advice and disarmed the Voion instead of anihilating them," Retief said to Jik-jik.

"Head-chopping hard work," the Ween agreed. "Us worked out a nice arrangement where one Voion assigned to each village to keep the sanitary drains open. It working out good."

"They like the jungle that way it is," Retief informed Longspoon. "No one gets any privileges unless he can manage them for himself; and prices will be controlled by supply and demand."

"I see I've underrated this fellow," Longspoon muttered to his aides. "He's obviously an exponent of some rather far-out economic theories." He adjusted a smile expressing the unspoken rapport existing between Men of the World. "Tell him that I've been considering the size of the development loan I'll be prepared to recommend, and I've decided that the sum of, ah . . ." He glanced at Magnan. "Ten million . . . ?"

"Twenty," Magnan murmured. "Per year," he added.

"Plus the military aid program," Underknuckle put in. "I'd estimate a hundred-man Advisory Group—"

"Twenty-five million per annum," Longspoon said decisively. "With a cost-of-dying increase built in—plus a sliding scale to compensate for seasonal fluctuations."

"Fluctuations in what?" Magnan asked alertly.

"Anything that fluctuates, dammit!" the ambassador snapped.

Retief nodded solemnly. "Did you collect the guns?" he asked Jik-jik. "All of them?"

Jik-jik wiggled his oculars uncomfortably. "Uh, well, Tief-tief, it like this—"

"Bury 'em, Jik-jik," Retief said sternly. "Along with all the captured guns. We agreed that firearms take all the fun out of fighting."

Jik-jik gave the soft squeal that was the Ween equivalent of a sigh. "OK; I guess you right, Tief-tief. Me and Tupper here already done a little scrapping over what tribe get 'em. I guess I rather bury 'em all than wind up looking down the barrel next time they a little intertribal rumble."

"What does he say?" Longspoon demanded.

"No loan," Retief translated.

"Oh, he's holding out for an outright grant," Longspoon rubbed his hands together. "Well, I think that could be arranged. Naturally, that will call for closer control: Say an additional staff of fifty—"

"No grants, either," Retief interjected.

"See here," Longspoon clamped his mouth. "If the fellow's going to be unreasonable . . ."

"All he wants is a Monitor Service station in a quarter-million mile orbit to ensure that no cargoes move between Groac and Quopp—in either direction."

General Hish made a choking sound. Colonel Underknuckle brightened. "That's reasonable," he stated. "Now let me see; the station would fall under my command, naturally; for a medium-sized unit, say thirty men—"

"There's one other thing," Retief said. "Terran honey will have to be added to Narcotics Control's list of excluded items as far as Quopp is concerned."

"Hmmph." Longspoon eyed Jik-jik sourly. "I must say this chap is a shrewder negotiator than I'd anticipated. I can see we're all going to have to tighten our belts and settle down to a long campaign before we can bring Quopp to readiness for membership in the Free Liaison of Organized Planets."

Magnan sniffed. "From what I've seen of these confounded rebels—that is, the freedom-loving standard-bearers of the aroused populace—they may never be ready for FLOP."

"Nonsense, Magnan; just give us a few more sessions at the conference table; they'll come around. I may even take time to absorb the language—not that I don't already have a good working knowledge of it," he added. "You handled the interpretation fairly well, Retief, but you missed a few of the finer nuances."

"I thought the nuances were the best part," Retief commented.

"Maybe you'd better invite these fellows along to the military ball tonight," Underknuckle announced. "After all, as the rebel leaders, we can consider them as honorary military men, even though they lack formal training."

"By all means," Longspoon said. "An excellent opportunity to make a few points; or rather, to implement our sincere and heartfelt sense of solidarity with the forces of popular aspiration."

"Oh, well put, Mr. Ambassador," Magnan gasped.

"It will be a gala affair," Underknuckle said. "A fittting conclusion to the excitement of the week, as well as a tribute to General Tief-tief and his gallant warriors of the Federated Tribes." He looked at Retief severely. "Tell 'em that; that'll soften 'em up."

"Remember now," Retief said to the callers. "No fighting at tonight's big social event. Colonel Underknuckle abhors violence."

"OK, Tief-tief," Jik-jik said. "By the way, we is heard they going to be some extra good stuff on hand . . ." He worked his oculars in a Quoppian wink. "I hopes that ain't no mere rumor."

"I'll personally spike the punch bowl," Retief assured him. He turned to Underknuckle. "He wants to know if he should wear his medals."

"By all means!" Underknuckle boomed. "Full dress,

167

medals and orders! A real military occasion." He gave Retief a cold eye. "As for yourself, sir—inasmuch as you're under charges for AWOL, I suggest you consider yourself confined to quarters until further notice."

Retief and Jik-jik stood together at the arched entrance to the mirror-floored grand ballroom aboard the CDT Armed Monitor Vessel *Expedient*, watching the brilliantly gowned and uniformed diplomats of a dozen worlds gathered under the chandeliers to celebrate the new independence of Quopp.

"Well, Tief-tief," the Ween said. "Look like all the excitement over for a while. I going to miss it. Cutting greens not near as good exercise as snipping Voion down to size." He sighed. "Us going to miss you, too, when you goes back to Stiltsville."

"You'll find that fighting in defense of peace will absorb all your spare energy, now that you're civilized," Retief reassured him.

"I is a great believer in peaceful settlements," Jik-jik assured him. "Ain't nobody as peaceful as a dead troublemaker."

"Just keep it within reason, or you'll have the Terries on your neck. They tend to be spoilsports when it comes to good old-fashioned massacres."

"Sound like a good tip; I'll keep it in mind." Jik-jik leaned close to Retief. "Beat me how that disguise of yours fool these Terries, even right up close. It ain't *that* good."

"Let me know if it starts to slip."

Big Leon appeared, uncomfortable in a brand-new black dress coverall and white tie.

"Looks like old Longspoon learned something while that rope was around his neck," he said. "Seems like maybe us traders are going to get a square deal now."

"Most people are willing to give up their misconceptions," Retief said. "Once they have them tatooed on their hide with a blunt instrument."

"Yeah. Uh . . ." Leon looked at Jik-jik. "I guess I had a bunch of wrong ideas about you boys, too. You looked pretty good charging in out of the jungle yesterday."

"You Terries done heap up a big stack of arguments yourselves. Maybe us ought to work out some kind of muual insistence agreement."

"Yeah—and while we're at it, why don't you boys come around the store sometime; I got a line of luminous neckties coming in that'll tie knots in your oculars . . ."

General Hish caught Retief's eye; he strolled over to join the small Groaci, now resplendent in formal kit including a gold fringe that dragged the floor and three honorary head-bladders, one with fig-leaf cluster.

"Really, Retief, I think you went a bit far when you banned Groaci shipping from an entire volume of space," Hish whispered. "I fear I shall have to insist on a relaxation of that stricture, as well as certain other concessions in the field of, ah, minerals exploration."

A waiter offered drinks; Hish accepted a clay pot of thick black brandy. Retief lifted a slender-stemmed glass of pale pink liqueur. "Don't confuse your terminology, Hish," Retief said. "I didn't ban your arms-runners and smugglers; it was the wish of Tief-tief, remember?"

"Come, come," Hish hissed. "Out of regard for a colleague, I refrained from advising your ambassador of the rather baroque role you played in the upsetting of his plans—but—"

"Tsk, tsk, Hish. I thought we'd settled all this earlier."

"That was before you overplayed your hand in presuming to dictate the terms of the Terran-Quoppina accord," Hish said crisply. "I think now that, all things considered—"

"Ah, but have all things been considered?" Retief sampled his drink, eyed the Groaci.

"Your departure from the role of diplomat to lead the rebel forces was a trifling breech of protocol compared with deluding your chief of Mission in his own sanctum sanctorum," Hish pointed out. "Still, if you arrange matters to permit a few teams of Groaci prospectors to pan a little gravel in the interior, perhaps I'll forget to mention the matter."

"I think you'd better suppress any impulses you may have in the direction of overly candid disclosures," Retief advised. "At least until after the Board of Inquiry into the matter of the downed yacht. The investigation is being pressed rather vigorously by His Imperial Majesty, Ronare the Ninth of Lily; it was his yacht, you know—"

"A great pity—but I fail to see what—"

"It was just luck that the missile that hit the vessel

failed to detonate and was found, nearly intact, wedged in among what was left of the stern tubes—"

"Retief! Have you . . . ?"

"The shell is in the hands of the Federated Tribes. They can't read Groaci, so they have no way of knowing who supplied it. Still, now that the evidence has been deposited in a safe place—"

"Blackmail?" Hish whispered urgently. "And after I risked my existence to get you into Ikk's office—"

"The famous Groaci instinct for backing a winner was operating that day," Retief said. "Now, I believe we agreed that nothing was to be gained by mentioning the unfortunate error that caused Groaci guns to be substituted for Terran propaganda—"

"If you expose me, I'll inform the Galaxy of your dastardly role in the affair," the Groaci hissed.

"I confess I might find that personally embarrassing," Retief said. "But my report will place all Groac in a very dim light—"

"Not so loud!" Hish warned, looking around.

". . . but we still haven't discussed the moral implications of your scheme to import from Quopp large volumes of parts for your justly famed transistorized Tri-D sets, mechanical egg timers, and electronic pleasure-center stimulators—"

"But Quopp manufactures no such components," Hish said weakly.

"Now, we both know better than that, don't we?" Retief reproved gently. "The Voion were to handle the harvesting, disassemble and sort the victims, and deliver them to the port, and you were to pay them off in armaments. What the Voion didn't know was that the entire scheme was merely a cover-up for something else."

"My dear Retief, you've gotten a touch of the sun," Hish whispered. "You're raving . . ."

"Once comfortably established, it would have been a simple matter to dispense with your Voion helpers and proceed to the real business at hand; turning the whole planet into a breeding ground for a number of rather rare species of Quoppina inhabiting the central regions of the Deep Jungle."

"What a perfectly fantastic allegation," Hish said

breathlessly. "Why on Quopp would we Groaci go in for breeding aliens?"

"Every creature on the planet—and every plant, for that matter—assimilates metal into its makeup. Most of the varieties in this region use iron, copper, antimony, arsenic, and so on. It just happens that there are a number of little-known tribes inhabiting the Deep Jungle on the other side of the planet who sequester silver, gold, uranium, platinum, and traces of a few other useful materials."

"Really? Why, who would have thought it . . ."

"You might have," Retief said bluntly. "Inasmuch as I discovered specimens in your luggage."

"You searched my luggage?" Hish's jeweled eye-shields almost fell off.

"Certainly; you carelessly left it aboard the heli you used to pay your call at my camp just before I was forced to blow up the Voion officer's field mess."

"I claim diplomatic immunity!" Hish croaked. "I demand the right to consult a lawyer—"

"Don't panic; I haven't confided these matters in anyone yet; I thought you might want an opportunity to smooth things over in a quieter way."

"But, my dear Retief, of course, any little thing I can do—"

"Here," a loud Terran voice said behind Retief. "I thought I confined you to your quarters, sir!" Retief turned. The portly figure of Colonel Underknuckle confronted him, the broad mud-colored lapels of his full-dress uniform sagging over his hollow chest, his shoulder boards drooping under the weight of gold braid. "You'll leave this vessel at once and . . . and . . ." His jaw sagged back against a cushion of fat, exposing inexpensive GI plates. His eyes goggled at Retief's bronze-black uniform, the dragon rampant insignia of a battle commander worked in gold thread on the collar, the short cape of dark velvet, silver-lined, the rows of medals, orders, jeweled starbursts . . .

"Here," he said weakly. "What's this . . . impersonating an officer . . . ?"

"I believe reservists are required to wear appropriate uniforms at a military ball," Retief said.

"A battle commander? A general officer? Impossible!
You're a civilian! An imposter! A fake!"

"Oh no, he's quite genuine," a mellow feminine voice
said behind the colonel. He spun. A breathtaking girl in a
silvery gown and a jeweled coronet smiled at him.

"And—and how would you know?" he blurted.

"Because he holds his commission in the armed forces
of my world."

"Your world?" He blinked at her. "Here, aren't you the
person who ignored my orders not to land here?"

"My dear Colonel," General Hish interjected, placing
a limp Groaci hand on Underknuckle's arm. "Is it possible you don't know? This young lady is Her Highness
Princess Fianna Glorian Deliciosa Hermoine Arianne de
Retief et du Lille."

"B—b—but I gave orders—"

"And I countermanded them, Colonel. I knew you'd
understand." She smiled radiantly.

"And, now, Colonel, I think you and General Hish
would like to have a little chat," Retief put in. "He wants
to tell you all about his plans for a Groaci surgical and
prosthetics mission to improve the lot of the Quoppina
wounded, past and future." He looked at the Groaci.
"Right, General?"

"Quite correct, my dear Battle Commander," Hish
whispered in a resigned tone. "And the other matters we
were discussing . . . ?"

"I've forgotten what they were."

"Ahh . . . to be sure. So have I, now that you mention
it." Hish moved off, whispering to Underknuckle. Retief
turned to Fifi, inclined his head.

"If I may crave the honor . . . ?"

"You'd better," she said, taking his hand and turning
to the dance floor. "After coming all this way just to lead
a charge in sheet-metal underwear, I think I deserve a
little attention . . ."

Great SF Authors

Great Science Fiction from Pocket Books

THEODORE STURGEON

A.E. VAN VOGT

JACK VANCE

KATE WILHELM

JACK WILLIAMSON

b SFG

Bestselling Novels from POCKET BOOKS